THE
RIDDLE
OF
ROSNARENE

By Paul A. Sweeney

Published by New Generation Publishing in 2013

First Edition

www.newgeneration-publishing.com

 New Generation Publishing

This book is dedicated to the memory of James Patrick Sweeney

Thanks for the inspiration

&

To all my family and friends thank you for your support.

Acknowledgements

I would like to acknowledge the input from a number of people without whom this book wouldn't have developed any further than just an idea .A special thank you to my Dad, James Patrick (Seamus) Sweeney, a man more talented than even he knew. A writer who has inspired me to write and I hope I have done him justice in attempting to follow in his literary footsteps.

To my mum Annie for her support. To Joanne and family for believing in me.

Cover Illustration by Samantha Bogle

Thank you to my family for the many hours I hogged the laptop, PC and computer and for their input to my life and my stories.

Thank you to all who contributed to this finished book either wittingly or unwittingly.

(Most of you unwittingly)

Finally:

The characters, places and situations in "The Riddle of Rosnarene" are purely fictitious and any similarity to names of characters, names of places or any similar story or situation is purely co-incidental.

Most of all thank you for taking the time to read this book and I hope you enjoy it.

Paul A Sweeney

Chapter 1

"I'm in the mood for dancing, romancing," blurted out of the tiny wireless on the bathroom window sill, as our Trina accompanied the Nolan sisters into a hairbrush in her hand. Another night on the town had been planned and she was in the middle of the preparation that went on every Friday. My other big sister Shauna was helping her curl her hair. She fancied herself as the next Vidal Sassoon, making the odd suggestion as to how a colour or shaggy perm might make vast improvements. I was in the bedroom I had to share with these two divas. The room was looking like a tailor's workshop with an array of different outfits strewn across the beds waiting to see which one will be chosen for this evening. I was having troubles of my own trying to decide which outfit would go best with the boots on my Charlie's Angel doll, jumpsuit or jeans decisions, and decisions?

Trina, which was short for Catriona, was the oldest of the three girls that resided at 22 Tarnat Grange. She was 19 years old and the senior member of the Corke household, a fine, tall, slender young lady with striking dark hair and hazel eyes, taking the bulk of her looks from her Dads side of the house. She was forever checking her clothes and hair. Shauna aged 16, was more like her mother; shorter and rounder in shape with glowing red cheeks and strawberry blonde hair. Mummy says its ginger, but this is something Shauna denied at every opportunity. A wannabe hairdresser, I had the feeling she'd change that as soon as she was allowed. I'm the youngest at 9 and a bit. I'm quite small with black hair cut in a bowl style, our Shauna says it's a bob but she got that from her hairdressing books. They call me Billy due to my resemblance to Billy Bunter from the comics though I was christened Sarah Louise Corke.

"Do any of you lot up there want a mug of tea? If you do the kettles boiled!" was the shout from downstairs as Mum plodded back up the hallway into the working kitchen. At 41, Mummy looked well. She had dark auburn hair and although she seemed to be on a diet forever, she never looked too heavy or too skinny to me. The years had been kind to her and she would look after herself going out regularly for walks. A casual dresser unless going somewhere special, a pair of jeans or track bottoms were the chosen attire with a printed T shirt most days.

I did my usual record breaking dash to the big kitchen table taking two steps at a time like my life depended on it. You see, when Mummy called you for tea it meant warm soda and jam. It was a case of first come first served in our house, and although I was small I could eat any of my sisters under the table any day, maybe because they were trying to look like that doll Olivia what's her face, you know with the guy with the big quiffed hair in that film? So they picked their way through most meals. "Looking after their figures so they could get a man," Granny said, whatever getting a man meant?

Granny lived with us in Tarnat Grange, a small rural village in the countryside of Ireland, after her own flat got burned down. She had left her tea pot stewing on the ring in the kitchen with the power on full and went to the bingo. Nanny is my on Mummy's side and the only grandparent I have left. The other three have all gone to the senior centre in the sky Dad says.

Back at the table Granny and me tucked into the warm soda. "Aggie do you want your teeth?" Mummy asked, as Nana sucked and pulled like a terrier pup at the crusty homemade bread.

"Catch yourself on Imelda; sure you know them new teeth are playing havoc with my gums, that young fella up at the clinic must have gimme somebody else's teeth." Mummy rolled hers eyes to the ceiling and shook her head. She had told me long time ago that Nana Aggie was old and not to believe all she would tell me. Sometimes she forgets things or talks to people who aren't there. Mummy sat down with her mug and Trina arrived in the middle of the floor, bobbing up and down in front of the mirror to check her appearance. "Dad home yet? she asked, " I was kind of hoping for a wee loan?" Dad was always a bit later home on a Friday, he'd stop off for a pint and was usually quite tiddley when he'd come in. Trina knew that was the best time to tap him for money. Dad duly arrived a few minutes later and we knew when Dad had been in the pub, he'd come in kiss Mummy on the cheek and say; "Well Aggie, I'm a lucky boy that your daughter took her good looks after her ma!" Granny would laugh loudly throwing her head back to reveal two perfectly

3

shaped gums, no teeth just gums. Trina got her allowance and disappeared. Shauna made a brief appearance to get a slice of the earnings before returning to our room where she put it into an old Quality Street tin, as she was forever saving for something. "Here you go Billy" Dad slurred, as he rolled a 50p piece down the kitchen table to me. I was saving my money too though I wasn't sure what for. I had heard Mummy and Daddy saying we didn't have much and I figured when I save enough I could present it at the table one day and all our money troubles would be over.

Granny wiped her chin where the warm butter had leaked off the soda, and made her way through to the parlour and settled down for an evening's television, where she would chat away to Bruce Forsyth and co until bedtime. I too made myself scarce, going back up to my room to complete the transformation of Kate Jackson. She was my favourite and as I only had one of the three angels then this was her. I'd have an early night as the weekend loomed and Dad always said "Never waste your free time doing nothing." Shauna would listen to the local radio before turning in, while Mum and Dad sorted their business downstairs, house keeping, bills and Dads reheated dinner before retiring to join Nana in the living room. Trina was always there when I woke up though I would never hear her come home.

This was how life was in Tarnat Grange, the Corke family were no different from any other family. Everybody knew everybody else, and a close knit group of locals were always looking out for each other. The weekends seemed to fly by. On Saturday mornings Shauna would go to Irish dancing classes with her friends and go into town in the afternoon. Trina would sleep late much to the disapproval of Mum, then get up, go out and usually wouldn't return till tea time. Dad would do wee jobs around the house before going down to the betting shop in the afternoon, whereas Mum, Nana and me would go get the weekly shop and had the rest of the day free to do what I liked to do.

Most Saturdays I'd go to Beth Mackle's house. Beth was my best friend, we did everything together. I lost count of the number of criminals we caught and the cases we solved as Tarnat Granges answer to Charlie's Angels. We'd play dress up and walked to and from school together right from P1. My mummy and her mummy had both the same picture on their wall; it was me and Beth at our first Holy Communion ceremony. I'd have my dinner in Beth's house and her Dad would tease me saying "I hear Tommy and Imelda Corke won the pools, I must get a loan of them." Her mum was really nice to me too. Beth would come to my house some weeks and we'd have a great time, putting on Trina's make up and using Shauna's hair curlers, and pretending we were grown ups going dancing. One Saturday Nana was minding us and decided she too would get dressed up with us and paraded around the room dressed as a punk rocker, her grey hair sticking up in spikes with Dads hair wax and wearing Trina's Doc Martin boots with her own long skirt. Dad thought it was very funny but Mummy was far from pleased.

Nana never minded us again, while Trina and Shauna banned me and Beth from their clothes and private stuff.

In the summer of 1980 Mum and Dad proudly announced that the Corke family would be having a holiday this year. It had been a good year at Dads work, and we could have a proper week away at the seaside and on the second week of August we'd be on the train to Kilrushden. I'd never had a real holiday before, just a day out with the school or a stay over at Beth's house was as close as I'd got.

On Saturday August 11th we arrived at Dillon's caravan site and for the next 7 days we'd eat and sleep in a rented 9 berth caravan with Dads brother Eamon, his wife Cassie and their son Barry. They were a strange family. Uncle Eamon was always complaining of health problems, he couldn't go for long walks as he had sore feet, sleeping in the caravan beds gave him backache and even the sea air affected his sinuses. Cassie was a large lady who enjoyed a cigarette, ample amounts of food and had a loud cackling laugh, while their son Barry was a spoiled little rat. At 11 years old and being an only child he had a digital watch with a musical alarm, a carry round tape player and got anything he wanted, he told us his school pals nicknamed him Baz. 'Big tickle' I thought.

The caravan was great fun. Cassie and Mum did the majority of the cooking, sharing recipes and the odd old wives tale. Nana would tell them how they should prepare things while constantly nursing her soap bag. Dad and Uncle Eamon would get the water, gas, put up a temporary clothes line and take walks to the shops for essentials, sometimes in their shorts and sandals. Not a pretty sight for anyone. Trina and Shauna lay out in the sunshine when there was any, while me and Baz played with the frizz bee or a ball. In the afternoons we'd all head to the beach were Nana would get the only available deck chair and talk about her dog Sheba running up and down the sand, then she'd get a bit cross when she'd call and she wouldn't come. Of course there was no dog there, but it was good fun to see other people on the beach, use their hands to block the sun from their eyes while looking for the imaginary dog as well. We would have a little time in the amusement arcade in the evenings and we got chips in a paper cone at night as a special treat. The sleeping arrangements in the caravan weren't great though. Trina and Shauna were in the bunks, the parents had the double beds while Baz, Nana and me slept in the U shape around the front of the caravan. Nana snored and broke wind a lot in her sleep, Baz made regular trips to the indoor toilet which was basically a bucket in a cupboard. It was only for number ones Dad said, but it made a lot of noise in the middle of the night. Kilrushden was nothing like Tarnat Grange, and although I was having a nice time I was missing home and my best friend Beth. On the Wednesday Mum got me a postcard to send to Beth and I used my savings to buy her a bar of rock and a shell necklace. On the Saturday morning we said our goodbyes to Uncle Eamon and his clan and made the trip back home. We had only been 40 odd miles away and for only seven days but I couldn't believe how quickly things had changed.

We got back on the Saturday afternoon, and while Mum and Dad did the unpacking I ran straight round to Beth's' house. As I got close I could see Beth at the window, and before I got to the door she was out to meet me. I was sure she was as pleased to see me as I was to see her, but she quickly ushered me away from the door and round to our den by the shed. Beth was upset and had been crying.

"What's up?" I asked.

"Nothing, nothing at all, how was your holidays?" Beth side stepped my question. I asked again; "What's wrong Beth?" This time she didn't hold back or attempt to deflect away.

"Oh, it's awful Billy. My Mummy and Daddy aren't very friendly to each other anymore, they shout at each other all the time and Mummy says she's leaving our house and taking me with her."

I was devastated for Beth but selfishly was thinking about myself; if Beth left I'd be totally lost. "Maybe they will change their minds and be friends again?" I said hopefully, but Beth's reply was adamant. "It has been going on for ages but Mum said I wasn't to tell anyone, I'm sorry."

She swallowed hard and continued; "Mums brother is collecting us on Tuesday morning and we're already all packed to go" she sobbed. "Daddy took some stuff in a bag yesterday and left and he didn't come home last night." I could feel a big lump in my throat and my eyes were welling up. My best and only friend in the whole world was going to be gone in two days; I must try and do something to stop it. I gave Beth a big hug and her present from Kilrushden. She smiled and said "thank you." I don't think she even looked at it; she was a million miles away. I promised to call back later, but Beth said she wanted to stay in with her Mum. I understood, gave her another hug and then ran home to tell Mummy the news in the hope she could do something to help. Mummy was as shocked as I was and went straight over to Beth's returning a short time later with the verdict I didn't want to hear, plans were made and Beth and her Mum would leave on Tuesday and move to her brothers house in Kiltamnaght, a busy, fairly large town about 82 miles away, but to me it was the other side of the world. I was so upset I didn't sleep much on Saturday night and although Beth and I played Charlie's Angels all day Sunday and Monday, I knew the inevitable was coming on Tuesday morning.

Mummy sat me down on the Monday night and told me that Beth's parents were having some troubles and Beth needed me to be strong, I was 9 and a bit years old, what did I know about grown up troubles? All I knew was this time tomorrow I'd be on my own for the first time ever.

Early on Tuesday morning I went to see Beth, we just sat on her fence not really saying much as her uncle loaded their stuff into a removal lorry, our Mums, visibly annoyed, helped him. I gave Beth my best Charlie's Kim jump suit and she promised to write to me. Mum and I waved them off, and in a flash she was gone.

Chapter 2

The remainder of the summer holidays were a dull and uneventful affair, and although I did get a letter from Beth it was very basic, just here's my new address, it's a nice place but I miss Tarnat Grange and my friends. We exchanged post once a week, then twice a month, then once a month until I would get the odd letter from Beth. I was back at school and feeling very lonely. I spent a lot of my time in my room playing with my own stuff and not mixing very well with the outside world. Christmas came and went with the highlight being Trina announcing her engagement to an electrician called Pauric Casey. He seemed to be a dead on fella, though he never came into our house much, well not after the time he called in coming from work and he had a belt thing on for putting his tools in and Nana thought he was a real cowboy. Dad liked him; he had a good job and came from a respectable family, so that was ok then. Shauna had sat her exams and got whatever it was she required to go on to study at a 'technical college of Hair and Beauty,' or something like that. I wasn't too up in results or what they meant, though Mummy and Daddy were over the moon at first, it then became a little overshadowed when she got accepted in some college in the city which meant that in September she would be moving out and into the student life.

Over the period of about 13 months, our house and home life had changed totally. Trina and Pauric had their own flat. Shauna appeared every other weekend with a bag of dirty clothes and her hair a different colour nearly every time. Beth would write the odd time explaining how she had lost her interest in Farah Fawcett and Kate Jackson and had replaced them with Wham and Adam Ant and all the little things we held in such high regard all meant nothing. I didn't reply as I felt I didn't know her anymore.

Daddy continued to work every hour God sent, Mummy got a wee part time job cleaning at the parochial house which left me, when I got home from school, and Nana, spending the afternoons watching reruns of old quiz shows, and the Sullivan's. I would do my homework and get the spuds peeled before Mum would get home. Then we'd sit down to dinner and more telly, and I'd go back to my room. It wasn't a great life, but it was all I had though. Sombre as it was it proved to have a positive outcome too, because when the results of my 11+ came in February I got to open the big white envelope myself, and I was more than delighted to receive an A!

Dad took some of the praise saying, "I told you Billy if you work hard you'll get the just rewards." Mum was very proud and we had a small party to celebrate, Daddy had to work so he missed it, but Mum, Nana and me had a good time, a few treats and new ear rings. I had already decided if I got the right results I wanted to go to St. Frances Convent. It was a brilliant school a few miles away, but I didn't mind travelling as the school bus stopped at the top of our road. Mum wanted me to go there too, so come September I'd start the new term at St Frances'.

Before the break for the summer holidays there was the small matter of my confirmation. "We had been practising for ages at school, in fact from after we did our 11+. You have to choose a confirmation name for the ceremony and I chose Mary, because that was Nanas second name, Agnes Mary O Hare. She was happy with that and bought me my prayer book and beads. Confirmation is a big day when you have to confirm your baptismal promises that your God parents did for you when you were a baby. My God mother was Bernie Gallagher, a friend of Mums who went to work as a nanny in America and never came back. She's an illegal immigrant now and can't come home otherwise she wouldn't get back into the states. The other God parent was Kieran Barret, he was my Dads best mate back then and they still had the odd drink together even now, though Dad says Kieran married a cross woman and he's under the thumb. I think she was Siobhan or Shidell or something like that. Nana use to say he was a nice lad till he took on that wee targer. Confirmation day was special. I had a new blue two piece suit with knee high white socks and blue sandals. There were flags up at the chapel and the Bishop was coming to Tarnat Grange. I was terrified of making a mistake, though I didn't have anything to do just say my bit with the others   when it came, and go up and get anointed with Mummy beside me. It was strange inside the chapel because my stomach was doing somersaults all morning in the build up, but when I came face to face with the Bishop I wasn't nervous at all. He blessed me 'Sarah Louise Mary Corke,' and I went back to my seat feeling as if I'd reached another milestone in my short life. Dad and Nana gave an approving smile and Nana leaned over and said; "You'd need to get outside sharp when this is over and be first in the queue to get your picture with the Bishop!" At that she waved her disposable camera and winked. We got the picture as well although we did have to wait a bit longer than expected and Nana wasn't best pleased. I had my picture taken with my classmates and then we went back home for sandwiches and I opened some cards; a fiver from Uncle Eamon, Cassie and Family, another fiver from Trina who was saving for her wedding in the summer, a tenner from Mum and Dad and a fiver from Nana which I wanted to give back to her but she insisted I take it. Dads friend Kieran gave me two pound when he called to see Dad and there was a card with a Kiltamnaght stamp mark. It had to be from Beth. I opened it, not knowing really what to expect. It had another five pound note inside and it said "Hope you have a great day, good luck and God bless," signed Teresa and Beth. Teresa was Beth's Mum. I was hoping it would say a little more than that, but I guessed Beth and her Mum had started a new life now, though I'd secretly always hoped they move back to the Grange someday. I was a bit down after opening Beth's card, but in reflection, she must still be thinking of me to send a card in the first instance, so that cheered me up.

Then Nana told of her confirmation day. She remembered getting all dressed up and getting a sixpence inside the apple dumpling. She had got her wires crossed, and had ended up talking about Halloween instead! Mum tried to correct her but Nana gave her that look, the one that meant the end of the conversation. It was a long tiring day but a good day over all.

The summer was overtaken by our Trina and Paurics wedding. They had been planning this for yonks and finally the day had arrived. It was a beautiful Friday morning and all the neighbours came over to see her off to the chapel. I was too old for flower girl and too young to be a bridesmaid but I had the new suit from my confirmation, got my hair done by Shauna and was set for a good day. Dad looked really smart in hired out tails, though he was in a right tizzy because he had cut himself shaving. Granny said, "Stick a bit of loo roll on it, sure nobody will be looking at you anyway!"

Mum had a new hat on. I don't think I ever saw her wear a hat before but it looked gorgeous, very posh. Shauna was the bridesmaid and she too looked very pretty, in a puffy pink satin dress, she even had a normal hair colour though the original strawberry blonde was a distant memory now. Shauna had brought her boyfriend along, a weird looking specimen who was the same shape from his ankles till his shoulders. He had a box suit on and one of them lace type ties, with an eagle on it. Shauna introduced him saying;

"This is Nicky everyone," and granny asked straight out,

"Have you not been well son?"

Nothing could take away from the bride however as Trina looked like a princess, a silver tiara in her long dark hair, her flowing white dress with sequins sparkling, she was a picture. Big flashy cars with coloured ribbons drove us to the chapel and Fr. Taggart did the wedding mass. He was the best man for the job seemingly, and Mum had got him through working in the parochial house. After the service we all arrived at the reception. Paurics best man did the speeches and he was very funny, although I didn't get the jokes but laughed anyway as I didn't want to appear stupid. Uncle Eamon was there complaining about the meal while Cassie was gulping as much free champagne and wedding cake into her as she could. Baz was there and although I hadn't seen him since Kilrushden, I still remembered how much a big head he was so I avoided him like crazy. He was easy enough to spot as he was sporting a mullet style haircut which had highlights in it, it was supposed to look like George Michael though it looked more like Mrs Quinn's old ginger spotty cat Nana said. Nana herself got a bit drunk that day. I think and she was up dancing with Paurics dad Peadar without her stick and almost keeled over a few times. The evening came to close with my Dad, his tie tied around his head, in the middle of the floor hugging my Mummy and the new Mrs Casey and all the guests singing Old Ange Syne and crying, all apart from Nana

15

of course who had her glass of stout and was stretched out in one of the booths, shoes off snoring like a baby.

The last week in August, and Mum and I were on the bus into town. Nana was staying home as she had a bug of some sort. We were heading to Walsh's drapery store to get my new school uniform. I was so excited; I'd never had a uniform before. Mr Walsh was an old man, I'd guess about sixty. He wore half glasses and had a bald head with a birth mark, it looked like a map of somewhere I had seen in a geography book but I couldn't remember where, and he walked with a limp.

"Morning Mrs Corke" he said as we entered the shop.

"How ya Brendan," Mum replied, "I ordered a blouse, skirt, and pull over for madam here, are they in yet?" He shuffled round behind the counter;

"Aye they're here alright, and I put aside a tie for you as well."

The St Frances uniform wasn't going to be a hit on the catwalk. The skirt was green, the jumper was green and the blouse was light green. Oh, and the tie was eh, green. Mr Walsh presented me with a white plastic bag with Corke written on it in marker.

"Away and try them on ya, there's a fitting room down the back of the shop there" he said. I did what I was told and appeared a short time later in the middle of the shop floor. My new gear fitted quite well although the stiff collar of the new shirt was cutting into my neck I felt like a real grown up. "They don't be long shooting up" remarked a lady who was waiting to be served next. Mum nodded her head. "Aye it's not that long ago I was changing this one's ass!"

I was a little embarrassed and retreated to the fitting room while Mum, Mr Walsh and the other lady continued reminiscing of their own school days gone by. After a wee walk round the town and an ice cream, we were back on the bus and back home in no time. Nana was sitting in the living room talking to the radio with her slippers and two odd socks on.

"Did you get me a bottle when you were in town?" she asked.

"You never said Ma" was Mums come back.

"Jasus Imelda, do I have to write it down for you? I was up all night wasn't I? Back and forward to the toilet I must have cut a track in the carpet." Nana went on "Every time I sat down on the bowl it was as weak as water and it hasn't thickened up much the day either!"

That was more information than I needed, and headed off to my room to put on the new uniform for Nanas inspection. When I got back, Mum and Nana were discussing Nanas bowel movements in more detail and trying to work out what had set her off.

"Well Aggie, what do you think of Sarah's new uniform?" Mum enquired.

"That looks well on you love" Nana agreed. A smile grew across her wrinkled face "You'll not be in need of a bra for a while yet though," she had a cackle to herself. "What school is that for now tell me?"

"It's for St Frances Convent Nana; you know the big school near Rosnarene?" I said fixing my tie to make sure it was straight.

"The Convent?" Nana snapped back. "What the hell do you want to go to the convent for, it's full of do gooders and holy Joes, they give me the willies them lot!"

I was shocked! "Do we have to hear this every time that school's mentioned Ma?" Mum butted in. "Your Nana, wanted me to go there but I wasn't accepted and she's been against it ever since. It's a great school, and if you work hard you'll do very well Sarah."

Nana slumped off into the kitchen still mumbling on about St Frances'. Dad arrived home later and assured me the uniform was a good fit and I looked very smart. It was then put on the hanger with a bin bag over the top and left in my wardrobe for the first day of school. I had sent a letter to Beth thanking her for the confirmation day fiver and to touch base and ask how she got on in her 11+ but her reply was brief, she didn't do the test and her Mum had decided the High School in Kiltamnagh was the best option for her. I asked maybe someday she could come to Tarnat Grange for a visit, but I got a direct No! Beth said her Mum would never go back not even to visit as it would have too many bad memories.

Beep, beep, beep, beep went the alarm at 7.00am. That was my cue to get up, wash and don the uniform that had been hanging in the wardrobe for the past 10 days. The first day at St Frances' was just two hours away. I had a bag of mixed emotions going on inside, anticipation, excitement and nervousness of course.

"You up yet Billy?" Dad shouted "Hope it goes well, and enjoy it, bye!" as he headed out the front door for another day in the mill. Mum was getting the breakfast ready when I came down into the kitchen; Nana was at the table in her dressing gown slurping porridge.

"Are you all set for your fist day?" she asked.

"Aye Nana I'll give it a go and if I don't like it today I won't go back tomorrow," I said jokingly.

"You won't get away that easy when you go there, don't you worry about that."

Was Nana trying to frighten me? If so she was starting to have some success.

"You'll be grand" said Mum, pouring the milk onto my porridge, I wasn't a fan of porridge but Nana reassured me saying, "It'll keep the heat in and the cold out."

"Will you be alright walking up for the bus?" Mum asked.

"Aye dead on, sure it's only up the road!" I laughed. "I won't get lost like."

Mum gave Nana her tablets and juice and I went upstairs to put the finishing touches to my appearance, I wanted everything to look just right. Back down into the kitchen for a final inspection, with the time now approaching 7:55am it was a kiss for Mum and Nana and off I went to get the bus.

When I arrived at the stop there were a few waiting, all of which were bigger than me. I didn't say anything just stood there in the sunshine. "Are you for the convent?" a voice said. I just stood and said nothing as I didn't think they were talking to me.

"Oi bowl head! Are you for the convent?" I knew now it was me.

"Bowl head!" I looked up and there was a quite a broad girl with a fringe and braces, "Are you deaf?" she asked.

"No" I replied.

"For the third time then, are you for the convent?"

I had it on the tip of my tongue to say, "Well I'm not dressed like this for fun," but I thought better and said "Yeah, It's my first day there."

The large girl laughed. "Thought so? I go there too, but you probably worked that out already from the uniform" she continued. "I'm a third year and the only one at this stop that goes to the convent, until now. What's your name?"

I stumbled through my reply. "Billy, no, I mean, Sarah. My sisters and Dad call me Billy, it's a nickname but my proper name is Sarah."

I so hoped she wouldn't ask me to explain and luckily she didn't.

"I'm Claire, with an "I" not as in the county. I'll show you round when we get there if you want? It's alright if you know how to play it."

I had no clue as to what she meant but figured she'd know best. The bus arrived and I stood back and let everyone on in front of me while Claire bulled her way through pushing boys and girls from St. Patricks out of her way. They too got on here as the bus passed by both schools on the way. There looked like one or two first timers going there as well today, one boy for sure was a first timer, his blazer too long in the sleeves and his face the colour of death. By the time I got on the seats were all gone this was the last stop the bus made before going into Rosnarene.

"Hey bowl head, you'll need to be quicker than that in the morning or you'll never get a seat!"

It was Claire again, her chubby hands cupped to her mouth to make the sound louder. She was in a seat beside another St. Pat's girl, who was squashed against the window, although I don't think it was intentional, just that Claire required a bit of space to spread out.

The bus trip wasn't very long and before I knew it we had arrived. Claire came pushing past;

"C'mon then, see ya later Dennis!" she said to the driver before disembarking, he just smiled. I clambered down the steps and the bus doors shut and it drove away, leaving about six or seven of us outside the green railings of St Frances Convent for Girls. Other buses had let other pupils off and some had walked, while more were being dropped of in cars. We walked up through the gates and onto a winding driveway that led to the main building, a grey structure with big windows divided into large rectangles by white window frames. It had a tower like spire top with a weather vain. There was a well kept lawn at the front with a statue, probably of St Frances I guessed, and I could see the tops of goal posts sticking up from down behind a mound.

"That's the pitches for P.E., do you play camogie?" Claire asked. I didn't know what she meant? I had saw Gaelic on the telly once but I didn't get to answer anyway before she went on;

"What's your name again, Billy isn't it, C'mon keep up. You don't want to get on the wrong side of Biddy on your first day."

I didn't know who Biddy was but it didn't sound right to me. Once inside we stood in a long, wide corridor, the floor was black and white square tiles like a draught board. There was a large crucifix hanging from the roof and it had a strange smell. I'd encountered the smell before in the parochial house when I went with my Mum to help her clean on my days off school. I was in awe of the place. Students were busily going in all directions like an army of green ants. Claire was hurrying along in front while I tried to keep pace and tried to look through the classroom windows as I went. We took a sharp right and down another corridor. The ants were getting a lot more in numbers and there was a queue forming in front. A Nun stood outside the wooden double doors holding up a sign with "First Year students" written on it.

"You go there Billy, I'll see ya later, good luck!"

Claire patted me on the head like a puppy dog and disappeared through the double doors. I walked over to the Nun and joined a group of nervous looking 11 year olds. After a little while she spoke: "Ok, listen up everyone, you are all very welcome to St. Frances' Convent. The school is run mainly by the order of St

Frances and a number of lay people whom you will meet at a later date. I'm Sister Bridget, your head of year. We will go into assembly now and you will line up quickly and quietly, there will be no chitter chatter and immediately after payers you will follow me and you will be put into your designated classes."

She spoke with authority and her tone demanded attention.

"Is that clear?"

We nodded as nobody dare speak to her. At that she opened the double doors and we entered a large assembly hall where all the other students were lined up like an army. The morning address was performed by the Mother Superior who welcomed all the students back after summer break, hoped they had a productive summer and were ready to start the new term with a positive mental and academic attitude. She gave everyone her blessing said prayers and left the stage. We were ushered out behind Sister Bridget, when I felt a hand on my shoulder, it was Claire. She whispered,

"I see you met Biddy then."

She quickly went the other way and I followed the rest of the group down the hallway and into a large room to be given my chosen classmates for the new school year.

Chapter 3

Once inside the class room we just sat where there was a space. I was right down the back in what appeared to be a home economics class. It had sinks and cookers and there was the odd mixing bowl visible. Three more Nuns came in and they gathered behind the main desk at the blackboard, clip boards in their hands, they chatted and compared notes. Sister Bridget spoke,

"The first year students will be divided up into three groups, 1a, 1b and 1c.When your name is called out, line up at the door."

She gave a list of names and the girls lined up at the door like she said. I wasn't on the first list. "Please follow Sister Maria" she said and off they went in Indian file behind the Sister.

"Ok, same as before, when your name is read out line up." She started a new list, but I wasn't on that either. "You can follow Sister Caroline." The second batch disappeared.

"The rest of you can find a seat and congratulations you're staying with me, we will be known as 1c!"

I looked for an empty seat and planked myself down beside a girl with jet black hair, she seemed ok from a first glance. Sister Bridget continued "My name is Sister Bridget and I have been teaching at his school almost 20 years. I studied here myself and I can highly recommend it. Throughout your time here you will learn many things, English, Maths, Irish, History,

Geography and others, but more importantly you will learn about you, about life and how to treat people in a way you'd expect them to treat you."

That sounded fair I thought. She went on;

"I want you to turn to the person next to you and introduce yourself. We will then take it in turn to stand up and introduce the person you've just met, each student will introduce their partner."

I was a little confused but figured I'll give it a try, so I turned to the girl next to me and said" Hi, I'm Sarah Corke but some people call me Billy, it's my nickname. I live at 22 Tarnat Grange. What's your name?"

The girl looked at me for a second and then replied; "My name is Niamh Cosgrove. I live at 16a Rosnarene Close. I don't have a nickname. I have a cat called Tiny and a brother called Louis; he's 13 and goes to St. Pat's."

That's plenty for now I thought, as I'll have to introduce her to the class and I'm nervous enough already. But when my turn came I remembered it all apart from the 'A' in her address. After introductions we got our timetable for our classes and the daily schedule. School would start with assembly and prayers at 8:50am, class would start at 9:05am sharp. There were three 35 minute classes before break time at 10:50am and it would last for 10 minutes. Classes resumed at 11:05am with three more classes before lunchtime at 12:50pm. The lunch break lasted 45 minutes and ended at 1:35pm and then the final three classes of the day took the time till 3:20pm, at which stage you would return to the assembly for prayers and out for the buses at 3:35pm.

It was a lot to take on board on the first day but I hoped I'd get used to it through time and was folding away my timetable when Niamh said, "Do you have any brothers or sisters, any pets and why do they call you Billy?"

I told her the Billy Bunter story and she found it very amusing. "I have 2 sisters Trina, who just got married in the summer and Shauna who is studying at Hair and Beauty in the city. I don't have a pet but I might get one, one day" I said hopefully.

"My brother is called Luke because my Dad likes the Dubliners. You know Luke Kelly don't you?" she asked. I just shook my head and looked lost.

"Have you ever been to Rosnarene before, have you got a favourite group or singer, what do you like to do at weekends?" Niamh barely stopped talking long enough to breathe.

"We go to the shops in Rosnarene on Saturday mornings, that's where I got my uniform for here from. I spend the afternoons doing different stuff and I don't really know much about music I'm afraid. Do you like Charlie's Angels?"

Now it was Niamhs turn to look lost. "I don't know. What do they sing?" she said. She clearly hadn't a clue who or what they were. Our chat was interrupted by Sister Bridget handing out jotters and text books. "You'll come to me for Home economics and Religion, Sister Martha does languages and History. Geography is Sister Kathryn. Science and Music are in the mobiles outside with Sister Josephine and Sister Margaret. Art is in the new building with Sister Brigene and the English department is also over there and Sister Ann looks after that. Miss Reid does the PE and Sister Anthony is a whiz with the maths. I am also your head of year and will answer any questions, problems or fears you may have. It will take time girls to find your way round and settle in, and remember Rome wasn't built in a day."

She had obviously done this before and had the knack for putting you at ease on your first day, I liked her. I liked Niamh too, although she asked a lot of questions and talked too much. I had a wee look around at break time and got shown to our other classes, picking up more books before lunch. Mum had packed me a lunch for the first day and I had just sat out on the lawn to enjoy the cheese sandwiches and orange juice when Claire arrived beside me.

"Well how's it going for you so far, what class are you in?" she asked as she tucked into a bag of crisps.

"So far so good," I said, "I'm in Sister Bridget's, I think it's 1c."

Claire laughed, "I knew you'd be in Biddy's group, she's dead on, I got her in first year as well, and she's a good laugh."

She seemed happy in the fact that she had guessed right. After wiping the crumbs from her jumper she stood up. "Chat to you on the bus home later, I got stuff to do, see ya!"

She headed back inside and I finished my lunch, taking another wee look around before getting in line to go back in for the third part of the day. More class room tours and more books brought us up to 3:20pm, and before I knew it I was back in the assembly hall. Mother Superior reminded the first year groups that school starts properly tomorrow before ending the day with prayers. We all left the assembly in an orderly fashion and sorted half trotted down the long corridor, the Sisters voice roaring "Walk" every two minutes. Outside the doors and down the school drive, I had been accompanied by Claire about half way down the tarmac, "C'mon Billy, you're going get no seat going home either" she shouted as she belted past.

"Which bus is it?" I was running but there were 6 or 7 buses parked at the bottom of the lane.

"The one with the black wheels" Claire laughed. Her backside wobbled from side to side as she knocked students out of the way like skittles. "Bus 8, c'mon bowl head!"

I could never keep up but I was able to get through the gaps in the crowd that Claire's large frame was making. I got to the stop and found the number 8 bus. I hauled myself up the steps and to my delight there were free seats, Claire will be pleased with me this time I thought. I plonked down in the seat, a little out of breath but I couldn't see Claire anywhere. Out the window I could see Niamh, who could walk home. I waved and she mouthed, "See you tomorrow." I nodded my head in agreement. The bus was filling up now and as I settled into the window seat, a tall thin girl arrived beside me.

"Move it twerp!"She gestured with her thumb. "I sit here; Bronagh and I always sit in the first seat so shift it!" I said sorry I didn't know and lifted my bag to get up.

"Where you going Billy?" a familiar voice said, I knew it was Claire.

"I sat down here and didn't realise that these girls sat here all the time, so I'm moving."

The tall thin girl stood by with her arms folded.

"You park it back down where you were and don't listen to her, there are no special seats for anybody it's first come, first served and there are no names on them so. You can go get your own seat!" Claire said to her.

"Why don't you mind your own bees wax and butt out tubby, it's nothing to do with you!" was the tall girls come back.

"It is my business, this wee first year is my mate and keeping a place for me, so move it or I'll bust the two of you!"

I was getting a bit worried, by this time the tall girls friend had arrived on the scene.

"C'mon Colette, you wouldn't want to sit there now anyway after them nerds were sitting in it," said the thin one, shrugging her shoulders and throwing her head in the air. Claire retorted, "Keep walking and tomorrow I'll bring in a couple of straws and you can use them for leg warmers."

She sat down laughing loudly and squashing the leftovers from my lunch under her bottom. I didn't say anything; I just sat there under her right arm the whole way back to the Grange, listening to her tales of how

29

nobody messes with her on this bus. At the stop we both got off and said cheerio, Claire threw her rucksack over her shoulder and walked off in the direction of the mill hill flats. I cut down the side road home and a few minutes later I was back to base. Mum was still up at the parochial house doing the cleaning but Nana was home, as always the telly was going full blast with Celebrity Squares.

"Hey Nana I'm home" I announced.

"Oh how ya Billy, how was your first day then?" she asked.

"It was ok Nana, quite good actually, I met a new friend called Niamh, she's in my class she talks a lot but she is nice and I also met a third year girl called Claire. She's a big one Nana" I giggled, "We get the bus together at the top of the lane."

Nana got up and a small shower of crumbs fell out of her lap.

"Do you want a cup of tea, before our Mum comes home?" she asked. I explained I had the spuds to do and change my uniform but Nana said; "I have the spuds on so change your clothes and I'll stew the tea."

I went up and put the uniform on the hanger for tomorrow and arrived back in the front room, Nana came in with the tray and 2 mugs of tea.

"Did your women get the full house?" Nana was nodding at the TV.

"Eh I don't know, Nana I wasn't watching," she shuffled over to the coffee table.

"For God sake, I don't why I bother watching those programmes, there's never anybody on them I know, I never get any of the questions right and Bob Monkhouse gets on my wick!"

She handed me my tea. I told her all about my first day and about how I can't wait till go again tomorrow, I loved it at St Frances'. She just supped her tea and then said;

"Is wee Biddy Carson up there?" she looked at me.

"There's a Sister Bridget Nana, and Claire called her Biddy, maybe that's the same person?"

I waited on Nanas response but she said, "Aye maybe." She was going to continue when the front door opened and in walked Mum:

"You're home already Billy, I thought I might have met you but a wee stout girl told me the bus was away ages ago." I wondered was that Claire.

"It was great Mum, I was just telling Nana all about my new friends Claire and Niamh and Nana said she might know one of my teachers, Sister Bridget?"

Nana turned the telly up and shrugged her shoulders; I felt I'd said something wrong.

"That would be Biddy Carson probably. She and I were mates at school, and she went one way and I went the other, and look at the way things turned out for her eh?"

Mum took off her coat and went into the kitchen.

"Billy!!" she shouted. I ran in.

"What is it, what's happened?"

Mum pointed at the saucepan of spuds on the cooker.

"What the hell is that?"

I went over and lifted the lid to find 5 big dirty spuds, not washed or peeled and the water stone cold. "Nana said she had put the spuds on today."

Mum just leaned on the draining board and laughed. "Are you trying to poison us Aggie? She exclaimed. Nana appeared in the doorway.

"What's going on?" she said.

I asked Nana about the spuds and she said; "They wouldn't be ready yet sure I couldn't get the bloody thing to light I must of went through a box of matches. I meant to tell Tommy when he comes in that the gas must be done."

Mum said; "Ma the cooker is electric, do you not mind me showing you the switch on the wall?" Nana got a bit cross. "You need to be a mind reader in this house, you're chopping and changing every farts end, and I can't keep up with you half time!"

At that she returned to the living room and me and Mum started to get the dinner ready, properly this time. As we got to work on the dinner I was very interested to hear more about Mums friendship with Sister Bridget. I just asked straight out:

"Tell me about you and Sister Bridget."

Mum laughed, "That's a while ago Billy, near on 26 or 27 years ago. Me and Biddy Carson were at the primary school together and although her family were well off we were still good mates."

Mum continued to peel the spuds; "Just like you Billy we did our tests and were deciding which school we would go to. In them days it was pass or fail, no A's or B's or any of that malarkey. We both passed and our parents went in to see Master Herron about our future schools. He was the head of the primary. They also would like to make suggestions as to what they would like. Your Nana was dead set on me going to St Frances and Biddy's Mum was the same."

Mum put the spuds on the cooker and went and sat at the table drying her hands with the tea towel. "Biddy and I went up to meet the teachers at St Frances and I hated it. I think the Nuns frightened me more than anything but we did a small entrance test thing and I never tried at all." Mum looked a bit sad now. "I got some easy questions wrong and the result was that I fell down the pecking order to get in. Over the summer months the letters came out to say who got a place and who would go to St. Patricks or St. Marys and mine said 'I regret to inform you that Imelda O Hare was unable to obtain a place at St Frances Girls Convent, Rosnarene.'"

I couldn't understand why Mum just didn't tell Nana she didn't like it so I had to ask;

"What did Nana say? Was she mad?"

Mum wiped her eye. "Nana was furious Billy. I knew she would be. She went up to St Frances' and told them it was a mistake, then started saying that Biddy Carson got in because of who she was and if our family had money then I'd get in too, they only wanted the ones that had something up in Rosnarene and the O'Hare's aren't good enough."

I was still confused as to why Mum didn't tell Nana the truth but she then went on;

"Nana wanted me to go to St Frances and I didn't want to go. I couldn't tell her that because she would have been so disappointed in me, this way it wasn't my fault and Nana wouldn't blame me." Getting up from the table Mum said, "That was a long time ago Billy and although I'm not proud of what I did, I turned out ok eh? That's why Nana has a problem with the school and I'd prefer to keep it that she doesn't find out the truth."

I didn't know what to think or feel. Mum was keeping a secret from Nana all these years and then again why did she think she had too? Mum said; " I don't want you to feel that you have anything to prove Billy by going to St Frances and if you don't like it, don't be afraid to speak to me, ok?" She had a little smile, "If you get a chance tell Biddy or Sister Bridget as she is now that Imelda said Hello."

I got a strange feeling that Mum had got rid of a large weight of her mind something she had bottled up for a while, she had an expression of freedom from something and I got to say I was pleased for her. Dad arrived home from work and after retelling my first day story for a third time I went up to my room and got out some old rolls of wallpaper and started backing me books and getting ready for day two at Rosnarene.

Next morning I was back on the bus with Claire. We both had a seat though, not together and went through the same ritual as the day before, only after prayers in the assembly we just went straight to class. 1c was English first two periods and then History, a wander round at break time, Maths and double Home Ec' a nice lunch from my plastic tuber ware box and finish the day with Science, Geography and Irish.

Day two over and I was happy enough. More books to back of course, more wisecracks from Claire as she continued to take the Mick out of me from time to time but again she was keeping a watchful eye on me as well, and another million questions from Niamh.

Friday soon came round and I was spending the last two periods in Home Economics. We were making a Shepherds Pie. I had the Green piny on me and was following the instructions in the booklet. It looked like mince and spuds to me with even more mashed spuds on the top. Mid way through dicing my carrots and Sister Bridget came to check on my progress;

"How are you getting on? Need any help?" she asked.

"I think its going ok so far," I said.

"How are you settling in at the convent? It's probably all very new to you, have you made any new friends?" I told her about Niamh and Claire and how I was likening it alright, though I had got lost a stack of times. Sister Bridget laughed, "I'm here 20 years and still get lost the odd time, its good you've made a few friends already. It took me a long time to settle here so you're doing better than me already."She went on; "Niamh is the wee black haired one you sit beside but I can't recall Claire?" I said "Oh Claire isn't in this class, she's a third year and we met on the bus."

Sister Bridget was stirring my mash. "A third year eh, and you met on the bus? So I'm guessing you live a fair bit away from here?"

I told her I lived in Tarnat Grange with my Nana, Mum and Dad. I couldn't resist the opportunity to say; "My Mum is Imelda Corke she used to be Imelda O Hare she said she knew you?"

Sister Bridget turned and her face lit up. "You're never Imelda O Hare's girl? How is your Mum keeping? What's she doing with herself these days?"

I thought Sister Bridget asked nearly as many questions as Niamh. "Mum works twice a week in the parochial house for Fr Taggart and she's keeping rightly. She has her hands full with Me, Nana and Dad to look after, and at the weekends our Shauna comes home from University with a pile of washing."

Sister Bridget sat down. "It's a small world. All this time Mello was living just a few miles away."

She was just thinking out loud while I went and put my masterpiece in the oven. When I returned she had moved on to Niamh who was having a lot of trouble with her pie. She had put the mash in first and then the mince on top and then more spud mash. It looked like a dogs dinner but Sister Bridget had a wee laugh and helped her saying, "It's like the Generation Game but we'll get it sorted won't we Niamh?" Niamh was lost for words, I hadn't seen that before.

3:20pm and the bell signalled the end of the academic day, so after prayers in the assembly it was the daily hundred metre dash for bus 8, today's race even more tricky with a Shepherd's Pie in my hands. I was soon walking back down the lane to the house and luckily so was the pie, after Claire had threatened to scoff it on the bus but settled for half a Toblerone from some young boy. Once in the back door I yelled, "Hello, Nana, Hello!" There was nothing, no reply.

"Nana" I shouted even louder but still nothing. I looked in the living room, the kitchen and in the hallway but there was no sign of Nana. I was frightened. I ran upstairs but Nana's room was empty. I was about to run to the parochial house and get Mum when I heard;

"You can't hurry love when you're putting on weight....."

I pushed open my bedroom door and there was Nana in Dads suit, the trouser legs wrinkled round her ankles and a pair of dark glasses. She was sitting on the side of the bed with Shauna's headphones on, singing into half box of cotton buds and looking at herself in the mirror. I waved and waved but to no response. I didn't want to go and tap her on the shoulder in case I'd give her a heart attack. I shut the door and went back downstairs and started my homework and waited on Mum, no need to peel the spuds today as Dad would be late at the pub, and Shauna would look after herself at whatever time she'd appear from the city. Mum, Nana and I would be having the Shepherd's Pie I had made. Mum arrived about 4:15pm and I told her about Sister Bridget and all about how she remembered Mum and was asking after her and that. Mum was chuffed, I could see that, but changed the subject immediately when Phil Collins came down from upstairs.

"Where have you been Aggie, were you up resting yourself?" Mum asked Nana.

"Chance would be a fine thing, I was up there throwing the clothes off them beds and opening the windows for a while to let the stink out, will Shauna be home soon?" Nana enquired.

"I couldn't tell you Ma, why what are you looking Shauna for?" Mum said as she took out the saucepan.

"There's a pair of them ear muff things up in that room and they're broke, the wee metal thing is pushed into the wireless too far and it won't come out. I was going to put them away for her but I don't want to touch them in case I'd get the blame for breaking them!"

Nana was such a wee liar. I knew that but thought I'll keep out of it.

"Grab a chair Nana and sit up to the table, you too Mum I've got a surprise for you."

I delved into the plastic bag and out come the Shepherd's Pie in a foil carton.

"God you girl ya, Chinese?" said Nana. "I hope it's not that green curry though, it cuts a track through me." I saw a smirk on Mums face.

"It's Shepherds' Pie Nana, I made it at school and I thought you'd like to try a bit?"

Nana was distinctly disappointed. "That will do instead" she said pulling out her chair. I heated up the carton then dished out the pie and we all tucked in. I thought it was ok. Mum said;

"It's tasty but you could do with a bit more onion or carrot maybe, but it's very good for your first try."

Nana shovelled it in like it was the last bite on earth. "Well Nana what do you think?" I asked. Nana wiped her chin with the table cloth.

"Aye it wasn't bad now, Fanny Craddock better watch herself or you'll steal her show."

I hadn't a notion as to who that was but Mum assured me it was a compliment.

Shauna came home from college raving about the big city and skinny Nick shortly followed by Dad with his usual Friday wobble and the handing out of the money, Nana retired to the living room for more telly, and I helped Mum with the washing up.

Chapter 4

"Billy, what have you done to my Hi-Fi?" Shauna screamed from upstairs.

I knew who the guilty party was but said I didn't know a thing about it. If I had said; "Nana was up here today dressed like a scarecrow in Dads suit and singing Phil Collins songs with the earphones in, who would have believed me eh?"

It didn't matter, Shauna had it fixed in no time and Nana was off the hook. I was telling Shauna all about St Frances' though I don't think she heard a word; she just kept saying, "Right, that's great, sounds good." Then she would tell me about the university and her boyfriend Nick, yuk! I didn't like boys ever since wee Johnny Trainor tried to kiss me one day we were playing Charlie's Angels. He ran home to his Ma with a sore ear that day- he didn't try that again in a hurry. Nana said I should have kicked him somewhere that you can't stick a plaster.

I had arranged to meet Claire on Saturday just for a walk about and she promptly called at our house at half one. Mum invited her in and we sat and had a glass of mineral while Mum found out all about Claire.

"You're from the Mill Hill then?"

Claire was so polite "Yes Mrs Corke, there's Mummy, Daddy and my sister Paula who's at nursery school," she said as Nana came in, still in her housecoat.

"Is that kettle boiled Imelda? I'm choking for a mug of tea." Nana looked at Claire "Hello there and who are you then?"

I jumped in; "Nana this is Claire."

I paused. This was the first time I realised I didn't even know Claire's second name.

"Doherty, I'm Claire Doherty, I live up by the Mill Hill," Claire said.

"Oh I used to go courting up the Mill Hill many moons ago," laughed Nana, "Long before your Dad came on the scene, God rest him." Nana looked at Mum "Are you making a cup of tea Imelda or what? There's no chance of me drowning, and if there's any of them Jaffa cakes left I'll try one."

We left them to it and headed out for a walk. It was a nice day and we just wondered round the Grange and went up by the park, had a go on the swings and over to the slide. It was funny because Claire was too wide for the kids slide but she had a go anyway.

"Something funny?" she said angrily. I turned round and there were two boys on the roundabout and one of them was sniggering. I had seen one of the boys on the bus during the week, the other was much younger and it was he who was laughing.

"He's only messing with you" said the older boy.

Claire was very cross. "He had better button it or he'll get a smack." She gave him the dagger eyes. "Mickey, wise up or I'll tell Dad!" The wee lad paid no attention; "I'm Colin Thompson and that's my wee brother Michael, every Saturday it's a decent day I get lumbered with him, he's harmless to be fair, he's just not very mature."

Claire was taken by Colin; "I know who you are, I've seen you on the bus, you go to St Pats don't you? You must be a second year?" she asked.

"I'm a third year actually, same as you. I've seen you round the Grange a few times, sometimes with a wee small child?" Claire nodded:

"That's our Paula, she's just coming four, are you stalking me or what then?"

At that Michael piped up, "You're hard to miss!"

Colin gave him a push, "Right that's it you're going home; you're a cheeky wee devil."

He got off the roundabout. "I'll see you round girls, maybe on the bus."

Taking his brother by the scruff of the neck he frog marched him out the gate and out of sight. Claire sat down. "He's nice isn't he and very friendly," she said. I poked her in the arm;

"Oooo Claire fancies Colin!" Claire's face was going red.

"I do not, I just think he's nice that's all, and don't get any ideas about telling it on the bus on Monday. I've only known you a week and I would hate to have to kick your butt already!"

I wouldn't say a word but I knew she did fancy Colin. After another spin on the roundabout we went our separate ways. When I got home, Nana was in the kitchen watching horse racing on the portable.

"I couldn't win a blooming argument" she said throwing rolled up dockets on the table.

"Where were you at the day Sarah?" Nana always called me Sarah; "that's what she was christened isn't it" she'd say.

"I just wandered round Nana and then went to the park for a go on the swings, and guess what Nana, Claire met a boy called Colin Thompson and I think she fancies him."

Nana laughed, "Did you not get a man?"

I was blushing; "Nah, I'm not into boys Nana thank you."

Nana came back. "That's what your Ma used to say too and now look at her."

I made a cuppa and went up to me room. It looked like a bomb had hit it. Shauna's stuff was all over the place, so I did a bit of tidying up and had me tea before hitting the sack. Sundays in the Grange were always the same, Mum would put the dinner on and we'd all go to last mass. Nana would have to get up near the front to be seen and then would ridicule what she called "The busy bodies," up giving out communion. She would only take communion from the priest and nobody else. Nana had old school beliefs, only those who had blessed hands should do that sort of thing, and maybe she was right. After mass and Sunday lunch Dad would get the papers, Mum would sit down and watch a film, Shauna would do Nanas hair before getting her gear together and heading for the bus back to Uni and I'd do my homework and get whatever I needed ready for Monday morning. We'd watch "Bullseye" in the evening and after "Songs of Praise." I'd be up in my room for a while before turning in and looking forward to another week of the same.

The weeks and months went by and I settled into school life at St Frances'. I got on well with the Sisters and teachers, and after the initial problems on the bus I managed to secure a seat most mornings. Claire got very friendly with Colin, and although she denied it I think they were an item. They'd go to the youth club discos and Claire would ask me to go along too, but I'd make up an excuse because I didn't want to be a gooseberry. Niamh came over to my house a few times and we became good mates. I explained to her who Charlie's Angels were, and she introduced me to all the latest music. We would try out singing the words from her magazines when they came on the radio, but Nana said it sounded more like somebody was trying to strangle a cat. I had met up with another girl called Madonna as well but she lived way out the other end of Rosnarene in a place called Finagate. It was too far to go at the weekends but we hung about some times in school. We looked similar as Madonna had the bowl haircut too; Claire said we looked like two pieces of a dinner service. Mum continued to work away at the parochial house, and from time to time she'd ask about Sister Bridget and sometimes Sister Bridget would ask about her. She even suggested calling around our house one time but Mum, like me, made some excuse about having something else on that day. I think she didn't want Sister Bridget calling in case Nana would say something.

Dad worked away in the Mill and Shauna was well settled into student life. It was wearing round to Christmas when we were all summoned to the living room on a Saturday evening. Trina and Pauric had come over and had an announcement to make. We all had a good idea what the announcement was, but acted surprised when Trina said;

"We're pregnant, I'm three months into it and we're both very excited!"

Mum was crying and hugging Trina and then hugging Pauric. Dad shook Paurics hand and said; "Congratulations to you both, I didn't know you had it in you."

Then Shauna was in hugging and crying. I did my bit of hugging too but didn't really see the point of it all. Nana said:

"Three months gone eh, you didn't hang about anyway!

"Trina was suggesting names, "We were thinking Whitney for a girl or maybe Simon for a boy, but we are open to any others you want to throw in the ring?"

Mum said, "You'll know what to call it when you see it, the main thing is that's it's healthy and got everything."

Nana chimed in again; "Who or what is Whitney? What's it mean? Do you know if you call it Simon it'll get Simple Simon when it goes to school?"

Dad was away onto getting champagne out, the one bottle he had saved from the Christmas do last year at work and celebrating the good news. The party went on till late. They were singing away and thinking of names way after 1:00am. Nana was sleeping on the sofa, Trina and Pauric had got a taxi home and Mum and Dad had finally realised they would soon be Granny and Granda Corke. Mum seemed ok with it but Dad was insisting on being called just Tommy. I think Shauna must have had some champagne as well because she was back and forward to the toilet all night and one time opened the door and got into the wardrobe instead! I got to sleep late on by thinking after June next year I'm going to be Auntie Sarah or Billy, whichever the baby prefers.

Monday morning on the bus I was telling Claire the good news, and when I got into class Niamh and Madonna heard all about me going to be an Auntie in the summertime. Niamh said:

"I think I was an Auntie once, well nearly an Auntie. My cat Tiny had kittens and Mum said I would have to look after them but through time they were given away or died, so does that qualify as being an Aunt?"

Madonna just laughed. "Did you wash your face with your own spit and paws too?" she continued, "At lunchtime I'll get a saucer of milk for you." Niamh wasn't amused.

I had to wait until Tuesday after break time to tell Sister Bridget the news of Trina being pregnant. "Heaven help us, Mello O Hare a granny!"

I assumed Mello was nickname for my Mum Imelda, and went on to tell Sister Bridget all about the big party and the names they were thinking of. She was very pleased for Trina and Pauric and said I should suggest Bridget when I see Trina again.

The Christmas tests came and went, and in January the parents had to go visit the school for a progress report. Mum and Dad went and I waited at home. Nana was taunting me saying;

"Bad marks will lead to red marks," but when they got back I had received a glowing report, in a nutshell: "Sara Corke was a pleasant and helpful young lady who worked hard and contributed well in class, her attendance was good and she had faired well in Christmas tests."

I was very pleased. Dad said: "You're doing well Billy, I heard all about you and I heard just as much about your Mum too from one of the wee Nuns."

Mum smiled. "I was doing a bit of catching up with Biddy; she was calling me Granny Corke. I couldn't believe it when she said she didn't know we still lived in the Grange. She was going to pop in someday?" Nana stood up;

"To do what, gloat at how well she got in and to look down her nose at us?"

Mum got angry; "No nothing like that at all. Biddy Carson was always a decent girl and nothing's changed. She chose what she wanted to do and so did I; nobody holds any grudges bar you Aggie so why don't you give it a rest for once eh? I didn't want to go to the school anyway so stop pointing the finger at the school or who else got into it."

Nana's chin nearly hit the floor.

"If your Father could hear you now he must be turning in his grave. We only wanted the best for you and....."

47

Mum interrupted: "The best for YOU you mean. If you had of tried asking then you would have known what I wanted but nah you were too busy pushing and pushing!"

Nana just stood there. Dad and I were astonished. Mum had really let all her built up emotions out. "It won't change a damn thing. Trina didn't get the grades and Shauna didn't want to go to St Frances' either, but I should have made them should I?"

She went on; "Our Billy has got in and she's doing well and if that's what Billy wants to do then I'm behind her 100%."

Mum took her coat and went for the door.

"You hold your horses Miss, I didn't bring you up to speak to me like that and I won't stand by and take it from you or be under a compliment to you. From tomorrow I'll look for another place to live, somewhere I'll get respect. By the way that child's name is Sarah!"

Nana stormed out and slammed the door. She had tears in her eyes and so had Mum as she went out the other door, leaving me and Dad in complete silence. He turned to me;

"Just the two of us for tea then Billy," he said. Dad and I chatted for a while, but my mind was on Mum and Nana. I'd never seen them in such bad tempers and especially at each other. I started to think if I hadn't had went to St Frances' Convent then there would have been no trouble. Dad sent me to bed as it was getting late, Nana was in her room with the door closed tight and Mum was still out, I never heard her come in.

Next morning I came down for breakfast. Mum was in the kitchen and Nana's porridge was on the table. I asked after her but Mum said, "She'll be down in a minute when she stops sulking."

I ate mine and went back up to get ready. I heard Nana come out of her room and go downstairs but she went straight out the door.

"Billy is that you?" Mum shouted.

"No, its Nana, she's away up the lane in her Sunday coat with a small case Mum!" I replied, as I watched Nana from the window. Mum darted down the hall and out the door. I could see her try to persuade Nana to come back in, but she was having none of it and walked on. Mum came back and said:

"Billy, your lunch is on the table, have a good day and don't worry about Nana, I'll have this all turned round by tea time."

I hoped so because I didn't like to think of Nana alone. I went for the bus and Claire said:

"Hey bowl head, I seen your Ma up by the Mill, has she lost something?"

I didn't know what to say, but I thought Claire is my friend so I told her the whole story.

"Your house is better than Coronation Street, babies, bust ups and ol dolls leaving home."

Claire was trying to lighten things up a bit as she could see I was worried.

"Don't you worry, they'll sort themselves out and it'll blow over in no time. Oh I forgot to tell ya, my test results were rubbish and I'm grounded for a month. My

Dad says if there was less of young Thompson and more books I'd be better off."

Claire sighed as she pulled herself onto the bus with me close behind trying to look up the road for any sign of Mum or Nana, but there was nothing. That school day was a waste of time. I couldn't stop thinking about Mum and Nana and what was going on. The bus had barely stopped at our lane and I was off; "See you tomorrow Claire!" I shouted as I made for home, in through the back door. "Nana, Nana are you here?" I called, but no reply.

I went into the living room and Mum was there. "Where's Nana Mum?"

Mum was very upset. "She's gone Billy, gone for good. I followed her this morning to the bank, the post office and she took out every penny of savings and just went- got on the bus and went and there was nothing I could do to stop her."

Mum unfolded a tissue in her hand, she had been crying. She continued on:

"I apologised and said sorry but she wouldn't listen to a word of it. I said people say things in the heat of an argument, things they don't mean, but it was no good. I said you need me to look after you, your medical problems and that," Mum sniffled and said, "She turned to me in the street and said:

"Never disrespect or lie to your Mother, you'll only ever have one.' Then she shoved a package in my hand and went."

I couldn't believe my ears.

"Where Mum? Where did she go?"

Mum shook her head. "I don't know Billy, that's the worst part. I've tried Trina's, I've tried the B+B in town and even her bingo pal Elsa but she never went to any of them."

I tried to calm Mum down and made a cup of tea.

"Should we go to the police?" I asked, but Mum said there was no point. Nana wasn't a missing person she had left of her own accord and although we knew she had her moments she wasn't diagnosed as ill or anything.

Dad came home and Trina and Pauric arrived with stuff from the chippy. Mum wasn't in the mood for cooking dinner, and I don't think anyone had much of an appetite anyway. We wrecked our brains all evening trying to think of where Nana might have gone to, but we couldn't think of anywhere we hadn't already checked. It was getting late so I had to go to bed, but I prayed wherever Nana was she was safe and that she would come home soon. I was in the middle of my prayers when the front door got a knock. It was pretty late so Dad went to the door, I heard him say;

"Oh, hello Sister, C'mon in."

I went to the landing and looked down but I couldn't see properly, so I made an excuse downstairs for a glass of water. I shuffled past Dad in the hall and could see Sister Ann from the Convent coming in. Mum and Trina were at the kitchen table when Dad opened the door and said;

"Imelda there's somebody here who'd like a word with you."

Mum stood up as Sister Ann came in.

51

"Hello, Mrs Corke I'm sorry for calling at the house so late but I need to speak to you regarding Mrs O Hare." Mum sat down a scared look across her face.

"That's my Ma, Aggie, What's happened? Is she alright? Where is she?"

Sister Ann went on; "Mrs O Hare is grand, she is in the sheltered housing block but I think we need to talk."

I was still getting a glass for the water but nobody noticed, as they were hanging on Sister Ann's every word. "Make a cup of tea Trina, sit down there Sister and tell me what's going on?"

Sister Ann started; "Your Mum arrived at the Convent today just after the children had finished for the day. She was looking for Sister Bridget but she was away on a course so I asked could I help?" Trina brought Sister Ann a big mug and she supped her tea; "She told me that over the past number of days she had learned a few things and that she had to put some other things right. Mrs O Hare wants to move into the sheltered housing. She said that she is homeless and will sleep in a cardboard box if we couldn't take her in! Then she produced a roll of notes, I'd guess maybe £500 or more and offered it to the order. We refused."

Mum just sat there listening then replied;

"Let me explain Sister, Mummy has always had a problem with the Convent because she wanted me to go there as a child. I didn't try to get in, and when the news of my failing got to her she blamed everybody only me. That was the guts of 25 years ago, but now my own lassie Billy is at the school and yesterday evening we were up at the Parent night and I got chatting to Biddy Carson. I'm sorry, Sister Bridget, an old school friend of my own. When we got back there was a hell of a twisting match between me and Mum and I blurted out the truth. This morning she up and left with not a word till any of us."

Sister Ann nodded her head, "That explains a lot," she went on; "Your Mum said she had family in the Grange but not anymore. She was at the graveyard chatting to your Dad yesterday morning." Sister Ann smiled, "She said he was no help as usual. She then went to Carson's old house, but it's turned into a public house now, so she had a hot whiskey and then turned up at the Convent wanting to see Sister Bridget and to stay the night."

Trina butted in: "How could Nana say she had no family here, we're all here. How did you know about us then Sister?"

Sister Ann replied; "I took your granny in and after a wee cup of tea and a promise of a night in our sheltered housing she revealed your address. She told me of her grand daughter Sarah being at the school and about Trina having a baby. She told me about her dog Sheba and how she can't stop him doing his business in the house and that's why she couldn't bring him to the Convent's sheltered housing."

Mum had to laugh. "My Mum has wee moments when her mind wanders Sister, bless her. Sheba is gone many moons ago. She loved that old mutt and used to feed him at the table. My Dad, God rest him, hated that dog."

She looked at Sister Ann. "I didn't know you had housing at the Convent? Is it for the elderly or what?"

Sister Ann finished her tea. "We have a Sheltered Housing block of 6 flats down behind the Nuns quarters at the back of the convent, and there are 3 pensioners who stay with us at the moment, that's as opposed to moving to the old people's home which is quite a bit away. We take the ones who don't want to leave the local area."

I hadn't seen the block either, but Sister Ann continued on:

"The wee flats are grand, they're not a palace but they have a small kitchen and a bedroom, they all have security cameras and a night porter and they have them emergency buttons and chords throughout in case they're required."

Mum was relieved Nana was ok and asked: "Will she be able to stay there for a day or two and then we'll get her back home? How much is it, better still does she now that you are calling to tell us?" Sister Ann said: "Yes I told her I must inform the next of kin of anyone taking up residency. Three of the flats are empty so she is welcome to stay with us until you can iron out your differences. There isn't a cost as such, we are non profit and work on donations, although she is adamant she wants to see Sister Bridget."

Even I had worked out why Nana wanted to chat to Sister Bridget. Sister Ann got up;

"I had better get back, it's getting late. I have a couple of requests from Mrs O Hare. She forgot her tumbler for her teeth," Sister Ann smiled, "Oh and she wants me to bring up your TV remote control because the picture on the portable up at the convent isn't great."

Mum laughed, "That's Aggie alright, she would die without the telly, and she thinks our remote will make it better eh?"

Dad chimed in; "Nutty as a fruitcake."

Sister Ann and Mum went into the hall. They were both giggling like school girls, Mum was thanking her and apologising at the same time. I was very happy Nana was in a safe place, in fact everybody probably had a million questions but the fact that Nana was in good hands and being looked after brought a collective sigh of relief. Mum came back into the kitchen;

"Thank God she's alright, though why on earth she went to the Convent I'll never know. She's no dozer I can tell you, she knew there was sheltered housing up at the Convent which is more than I knew."

I asked: "Do you think I could call and see her after school tomorrow Mum?"

Mum frowned' "I don't think that's a good idea Billy, but keep an eye out for her though. I'll ring in the morning and ask about getting a chat with her and hopefully she'll have cooled and we'll get her back home."

The drama at 22 Tarnat Grange seemed over for the night and I returned to my bed and slept a bit more soundly.

Next day I asked Claire on the bus did she know about the sheltered housing?

"Aye, you're talking about the prefabs, they're old peoples flats down the back of St Frances. I was down there at Christmas with the choir to sing carols for the old dolls and old boys. There's only three or four in them. Why?"

I told her about Nana. "They're dead on flats like, bit small but alright."

I didn't say it but I thought a flat would be a bit small for Claire. Anyway I did like Mum said and went about my normal school day. I didn't go looking for the sheltered housing. When I got home Mum was working away in the kitchen:

"Hi Mum, I'm home, did you ring about Nana?"

Mum went on working like she didn't hear my question. I thought she may be still in bad mood so I left it and went upstairs and got changed. After I had finished my homework I came down to tea. Mum, Dad and I were having sausage and mash and thankfully Dad asked;

"We'll any word from the Fugitive?"

Mum's reply was brief. "I rang this morning and the Mother Superior said I should leave it for a day or two and then pop in, they're very busy."

Dad said; "And that's it?"

Mum tutted, "Yep that's it, short and sweet!"

I was confused and hoped Dad had another question coming and he had:

"So what's the plan now then?"

Mum shrugged her shoulders; "I thought I'd give her till the weekend and if she didn't appear home then we'd take a spin up?"

I wanted to see Nana now, but figured things will get better with time. I went up to Mill Hill and called for Claire, she came out and we went down by the Green water. That wasn't the proper name for the stream but the water was always covered in mossy stuff so we called it Green water.

"How's your granny then, is she still up at the prefabs?"

I nodded. Claire went on: "Do you get your own room now?" she said pulling a Curley Wurley out of her pocket.

"Nah, I don't want me own room, I only have to share at the weekends when Shauna comes home anyway, besides Nana will come home soon and then where would she sleep?"

Claire laughed, spraying me in bits of chocolate.

"Your granny might meet some old fella up at the sheltered housing and the two of them might run away together on their Zimmer frames!"

I didn't think Claire was serious. "How's young Thompson?" I said, "Any danger of you two running away?"

Claire looked at me strangely; "That kind of talk usually ends up with a slap bowl head, Colly is a dead on lad but we're just good mates!" she walked ahead.

"Colly is it now, very cosy indeed, has he got a pet name for you?" I asked.

"Nah, just Claire."

Around the corner came Mickey Thompson on his brother's chopper. It had to be somebody else's bike because if Mickey sat up on the saddle his feet couldn't reach the pedals.

"Hello girls, how are the three of you?" He circled around us. "Sorry I thought there was three of you there!"

He was always having a go at Claire for being big.

"Somebody take the stabilizers off for you Mickey, wow you are a big boy now, your Mummy will be pleased!" Claire said.

"Are you looking our Colin to go for a walk with you Claire?" he smiled "Do you want to hold hands down by the Green water eh? Oooo young love!"

Claire was getting angry. Mickey must have said something near the truth?

"Go home you wee dweeb and act your age, go and get your Mummy to change you bum."

Mickey went round again; "Hello there pin head have you got a boyfriend yet; probably not your no stunner are you?"

I thought great, now I'm going to get a touch;

"I don't like boys, they're tubes."

Claire joined in; "Aye and you're the proof" Mickey started to cycle away "I'll head on and tell Colin were you're at skinny, then you can swap spittle with him and I'll vomit thinking about you, cheerio pin head!"

I thought he's a cheeky brat. Claire just said, "Don't mind him he's a nerd, come on its getting dark." She was right so I headed for home, got me supper and headed for bed. Our house had such a hole in it without Nana, she tied it all together and although I didn't want to show it I really missed her. I'd guess Mum and even Dad might miss her too.

Chapter 5

Saturday morning soon wore round, and Mum and I were up good and early and ready for the bus into Rosnarene. No grocery shopping this week for us, we were on our way to the prefabs behind St. Frances' to meet Nana. We hadn't seen or heard from her in four days. When we got to the Convent, we went round the back and down the short walkway to the Convent proper were the Nuns stayed, there we met Sister Ann.

"Well, you found it alright then?"

Mum nodded as Sister Ann lead us a few metres past the main building and round into what looked like a mini village. The little houses looked like they were made of tin and were in blocks of two, and set in a U shape they were very close together. Sister Ann went to number 2 and pushed the bell. Out of a silver box on the wall I heard Nana say: "Hello, Who's that?"

Mum smiled; "It's Sister Ann, I've brought some visitors to see you."

There was a small pause and then a buzzing sound. Sister Ann pushed the door open and said; "There you go Mrs Corke, Good luck!"

We walked into a small hallway and she shut the door. I didn't know what to do next, and as we stood there another door opened and Nana poked her head around.

"Oh it's you lot, she didn't tell me you were coming, what you want?" she snapped before disappearing back into the room. Mum took a deep breath and we went in.

"Well Mum How ya keeping?" she said.

"Hi Nana" I joined in.

"Hello Sarah, are you well, how's school?" Mum sat down.

"Going alright Nana, this is a nice wee place you have." I said quickly. "Mum and I were looking forward to coming up to see how you were getting on." Nana glanced over at me.

"That's very thoughtful of you and your Mother, you needn't have bothered though I'm knocking round long enough to look after myself!" She got up, "Would your Mother like tea?" she asked me. "That would be great, tell your Nana" Mum said.

I was like an interpreter, a go between. They went on;

"Ask her would she like a bit of Swiss roll with the tea?"

Mum replied; "No thanks, still watching my figure."

This was awful, and then I had an idea. When Nana went into the kitchen, I said:

"Mum I'm going out for a bit of fresh air it's very stuffy." Before she could say anything I was gone. They had to talk to each other now there's nobody else there. I walked up by St Frances'. It was funny to peek through the big windows and see the draught board corridor completely empty. I waited for about half an hour and was heading back down to the flats when I met Sister Bridget; "Hello Sarah, what brings you up here on a Saturday?"

Should I say or not I thought? "My Nana lives here now, well she moved in on Tuesday but all her stuff is still at our place."

Sister Bridget looked surprised; "Is that the Mrs O Hare I'm going to now? I got back from the course and there was a message from the Mother Superior for me to call at number 2 as there is a new resident who was asking specifically for me?"

I shrugged, "I'd say that's her alright, her and my Mum had a big fight after parents night and she left home, we didn't even know where she was and then Sister Ann called and said she was here."

I told her about the frosty reception as we got to the door. Beeeep went the buzzer again.

"Hello, who's that?" said Nana.

"I'm Sister Bridget just checking in, you wanted to see me?"

Buzz went the door and we were back inside. Mum and Nana were watching racing and were talking, only briefly, but it was a start, Mum had got a better picture on the telly I think.

"Good Morning Mrs O Hare, I'm Sister Bridget, we haven't met before but I understand you wanted a wee word?" Nana stared at the Sister for a second.

"Who are you and what do you want?" before Sister Bridget went through her introduction again. Mum said, "Ma this is wee Biddy Carson!"

It was like somebody had told Nana she had won the pools, she just sat there with her mouth open; "Your parents must be so proud of you!" she stood up and turned the telly off. "You probably don't remember me but a few years ago I met you and your Mother in the street in front of a number of people and I let my bad temper get the better of me. I was so angry because your family had a few bob and you had got a place at the Convent, I told you never to darken my door again, and that my family were every bit as good as yours...."

Nana was getting upset, "That was a long time ago and I now know that all the money in the world wouldn't have made a difference. I wanted somebody to blame and so I went for your family and then the Convent. I have made my peace with the Mother Superior and now I want to apologise to you and your parents?"

Sister Bridget said; "I remember that day very well Mrs O Hare, but not because you were angry but because that was the end of me and Mello's friendship. We only ever spoke briefly after that and slowly drifted apart. My parents are both gone now I'm afraid, we moved down the country a little and after Mum died, Daddy was broken hearted and he went just 8 weeks after her."

Sister Bridget took Nana's hands: "They didn't hold any grudges Mrs O Hare and neither do I. People do and say what they think is right at the time and then think later," she turned to Mum, "Like Imelda did with that test paper that day, right Imelda?"

Mum was welling up, "That's right Ma. I was so sure you'd think I'm a disappointment to you and Dad if I had of told the truth so I took the easy road out?"

There was silence for a second but it felt like an hour the Nana spoke;

"Who the hell was I apologising to during the week then if your Ma and Da are in the graveyard? I spoke to some young lad at your Mother's house and kept offering me a drink?"

Sister Bridget smiled, "My Dad sold the house to Kelly's and they turned it into a bar years ago, that's probably were you were I doubt."

Nana sat down, "I must be starting to dote, I wondered because I said to myself there's some crowd in this house of a Tuesday dinner time. Sure If I had of known your parents had died I could've called with them up there in the graveyard when I was up seeing your Dad Imelda."

I was totally lost in the whole emotion of it all. Nana apologised to Mum for pushing too hard as a child and not being able to see it wasn't what she wanted. Mum was apologising to Nana for raising her voice and speaking out of turn, Sister Bridget had sorted our family out in 10 minutes flat. I was so happy to see all of them just sitting chatting about old times round the Grange and Rosnarene. Sister Bridget shook Nana's hand again and then left to go and unpack her things. She assured Nana all was forgiven, that just left Me, Mum and Nana.

"Will you come back up home with us now Aggie? We all miss you around the place," Mum asked Nana.

"Imelda love, I realised over the past few days that you have enough to do without me, you have two young girls and Tommy to look after plus a decent house to keep. I'm ok here and I get looked after well and it's my own wee place, until I burn it down or something" she laughed, "You're only five minutes down the road and sure and you can call anytime, maybe I'll take the odd trip the other road sometimes too if I'm welcome?"

Mum and Nana hugged each other. I was crying but I wasn't sad. "There's something you can do for me Sarah?" said Nana.

"Yes Nana what is it?" I asked,

"Do you see straight across the road, in the other flat? That's Winnie's flat. Now she was over here on Thursday night and we watched the telly and had tea and from she left I can't find my good teeth..."

Mum went to interrupt:

"Wait till I finish. Yesterday morning I got up here and had a bit of breakfast, just a bit of Veda loaf but I couldn't enjoy it, I only had my talking teeth in and I have searched this place up and down and I can't find my eating teeth?"

I was lost, "How many teeth do you have Nana? What is it you want me to do again?"

Nana looked up to the ceiling, "Jasus child dear are you not listening to me, I have eating teeth and talking teeth, but I can only find my talking teeth, look these ones!"

At that Nana took out her top set of teeth, she went on "Winnie must have stolen my eating teeth on Thursday night I tell you!" Nana put her teeth back in and said, "Yesterday at dinner time the taxi come for Winnie to go to the physiotherapy and out she come waving and smiling over at me, she was smiling at me with my own teeth!"

Mum walked into the hallway and I could see her shoulders going up and down as she was laughing but Nana was serious; "Would you look out for her during the week maybe if she's about and look at her teeth. Would you know my eating teeth if you seen them?"

Mum was nodding at me to say yes so I said, "I'll keep the eyes peeled Nana, and if I spot your teeth I'll get them for you."

Mum said, "Right Aggie we'd need to make tracks for home here. Is there anything we can get or do for you?"

Nana walked us out to the door; "Nah there's nothing I need and if there was then Charlie would get it, he's the night watch man, he'll be in about half seven and check we're alright and he's there until morning, just the push of a button away." She paused, "I'll tell you what though, if Sarah wants to pop in after school some day during the week that would be ok, the days you're at the Parochial. I have one or two wee jobs need doing around here."

I hoped Mum would say yes and she said, "Up to you Billy?"

"I'll check if it's ok with Sister Bridget and if it is I'll call and tell you Nana."

At that a taxi pulled round and an old lady got out, the driver helping her to the door next to Nana's. "Great that is just what I need," said Nana, "that's hairy Mary away in, she's as deaf as a stone, she had the telly blaring the other evening and I went in to tell her to turn it down a bit. Och God help her she's lovely wee woman, she made me and her mugs of tea and when she put a new battery in her ear thingy she was alright. People can't help how they look, but she has a big bunch of hair growing out of her chin like a Connemara goat."

Mum looked at her watch, "Mum we're going to have to run to get the bus, ring if you need anything, cheerio."

Nana waved, "Aye Cheerio!"

Me and Mum must have broke the speed limit for people running, if there was one, but we did catch the 4:00pm back out to Tarnat Grange, and although we weren't taking Nana back with us, I think Mum was relieved the argument was settled and that Nana was happy and enjoying her little bit of independence. Deep down I wanted Nana at home, but I think I was happy for her too.

It was still quite a bit different without Nana living at our place, but I was allowed to call with her the odd time and Mum and I would visit her at weekends. Every fourth weekend she would come to us for Sunday lunch and get Shauna to do her hair before going back to her own place.

I was doing well at school, and one Friday afternoon I went round to Nana's but she had gone to town in the taxi with Mary. So I decided I'd go on home, but on the way out I met Sister Bridget and she told me Nana usually came back about 4:00pm and if I wanted to wait then I could help her lock up the school and generally tidy up a little. I was happy to help, and it didn't take long as the cleaning ladies had done the most of it already.

"Just the Mothers office and that's us Sarah," Sister Bridget said, as we walked into a large drawing room with a big wooden desk, long dark velvet curtains and plush carpet. This was the Mother Superior's head office. I had never been in here before which was good, because the only ones who had been in here were in trouble of some kind. Sister Bridget locked up the files and checked the windows were closed then she dusted down the desk. She was putting some books away in a large wall unit;

"Is there anything I can do to help you?"

Sister Bridget paused, "Let me see, do you want to dust down the mosaic?"

I didn't know what that was but said, "Yes, just point the way."

We went over to the other side of the room and on the floor there was a picture of St Frances' Convent, it was made from stone and tile pieces which made it sit out like it was 3D. It was amazing, it was so real. "It's very impressive isn't it?" asked Sister Bridget. "That's my Dads handy work, him and two other men made it from local materials, stone from the Mill and slate from the quarry. He was a contractor and made it as a gift to the Mother Superior at that time."

I was still staring, "It's brilliant, really good. Your Dad must have spent a long time on it."

I was still admiring the mosaic when I noticed there was a piece missing at the entrance of the Convent.

"Is it missing a piece?"

Sister Bridget shrugged, "It was complete when Dad put it on display, but a piece went missing years ago and it never was replaced. It was supposedly taken by a student who had got punishment from the Mother but it was never found, so that's how it's always been since I've been coming here."

It sort of spoiled the picture, but it was still very pretty. We were finishing up when I saw the taxi go round to Nana's flat. "There's the taxi now Sister, may I go please?" I asked.

"Yeah surely Sarah, thank you for your help, tell Mrs O Hare I said Hello and I'll pop in later."

I went down and helped Nana in with her shopping, Mary came in too;

"Hello Sarah, how you doing today, how was school?" asked Nana.

"Dead on Nana, I was helping Sister Bridget do bits and bobs up in the convent."

Mary sat down, "Were you shopping?" I asked her.

"Shocking, what's shocking" she replied.

"Nah, I said were you and Nana shopping, you know at the shops?" I said a bit louder.

"What?" was Mary's next reply?

"Turn up thingy!" said Nana pointing to Mary's hearing aid, "You can turn it back up now!"

Nana turned to me, "She can't hear a bloody thing without that ear job turned up, and then she has to turn it down in the taxi because it interferes with the taxi radio."

I laughed and Mary piped up, "I'll turn this thing up a bit now I'm not in the Taxi then I'll be able to hear you eh?"

Nana just tutted, "Aye do that and save our voices, do you want a cup of tea Sarah or a drop of juice and a wagon wheel?" Nana enquired.

"I'll have the juice. Better still Nana you sit down and I'll make the tea. Do you take sugar Mary?" Mary was fixing her levels.

"Mary! That child is talking to you, God save us!" Nana shouted.

"What's that Aggie?"

I tried again, "How many sugars do you take in your tea Mary?"

She looked at me confused.

"Aye I'd love a cup, milk and no sugar."

We had got there in the end, so I went into the kitchen to make the tea while listening to Nana and Mary talk or shout about their days bargain hunting.

"I should have taken the cardigan when I seen it, didn't I tell you I'd forget it?" Nana said.

"Forget what?" said Mary.

"The cardigan Mary, do you mind the cardigan in Herron's, the black one with the stripes. It looked like an Everton mint?"

Mary said, "Nah Aggie, mince and tea, sure what kind of a mixture is that?"

Nanas reply was brief; "Forget it, ears for hanging glasses on!"

They were a great couple, and were good company for each other. Nana's mind would wonder from time

70

to time and Mary joined in the conversations, when she could hear them. We had the tea and wagon wheels before Mary said, "I'm going to make tracks and get the heating on for a bath and cut my nails."

Nana made a joke; "Fingers or toes?"

Mary replied; "Singing for crows, what crows? Sometimes I wonder what the hell your Nanny is talking about!" Mary laughed as she closed the door.

"She's a good old skin but deaf as a post. So you were up in the Convent today?" Nan asked.

"Yeah, I went in with Sister Bridget for a wee while just locking up and tidying, oh and we were in the Mother Superior's office Nana and she showed me the mosaic."

Nana said "What mistake?"

I thought Mary was still here:

"The mosaic Nana, it's a picture of St Frances and it's made from stones and slate stuff, it's very pretty and well put together." Nana started to put away some shopping,

"I got them on special offer." She produced two packets of wallpaper paste.

"What's that for Nana, you have no wallpaper?" I asked.

"Wallpaper? What are you talking about Sarah, I have no wallpaper, I think you are going doolally round this place, there's only me and Sheba that are near wise! Where is that dog?"

I looked again just to be sure:

"That's paste for wallpapering Nana, why did you buy that?"

She lifted the packet, "Is that not Lemon flavoured Angel Delight? I was going have that after the dinner on Sunday!"

We both had a good giggle at Nana's blunder.

"You were saying the picture is nice then?" she said. "Aye it's lovely Nana, but it's ruined because somebody who got in trouble at school stole a piece of the mosaic, it's never been seen since."

Nana gave a rye smile, "I know were that is, I gave that to your Mum."

I thought right, she's off again! "That's great Nana I bet they would like to have it back though for the picture?" She walked past my shoulder and said;

"Ask your mum for it then and she'll give it to you."

I followed her in and got my coat, "I'd need to go Nana and get the bus, I'll see you on Sunday, I'll come up with Mum." Nana switched on the telly;

"Right love, be careful going home and don't be too early on Sunday, cause I'll be getting me dinner at half twelve and there's no point in you and you Mum coming up here and looking down my throat, I wouldn't enjoy me dinner that road," she said.

"I'll let Mum know, I'm sure she'll be happy to hear that, see ya Sunday Nana, Bye!" I shouted. "Cheerio love," was the reply.

The months went by with very little happening or changing for that matter. Claire and Colly became more of an item and at the end of term Claire asked me to go with her to the disco in parochial centre, I always refused but this one was different. Colin Thompson had been meeting us up in the park every other Saturday, and I was always the spare sitting round on the swings while they sat and whispered sweet nothings. Then Mickey would throw a spanner in the works by calling Claire names or winding me up. I told Claire I felt awkward, and Colin came up with a brain wave of getting me a blind date, a blind date at 11 and bit years old! Mickey said the boy would need to be blind to date me anyway. If I didn't go through with it then all sorts of rumours would start going around so I said ok. The suspense was building up over a few weeks before the disco, and Claire was forever keeping me going about who it might be. Anyway the day arrived, and I had already checked it with Mum and I was good to go. Shauna was home and I got my hair done which seemed the rule in our house, when Shauna came home somebody got their hair done. It was the first time in my life that the bowl was missing, middle shade and brushed back, it added ten years on me but Shauna assured me it was very hip and cool. I had a bath and Mum got me a new flowery blouse and jeans with designs on the sides. I had my sandals on, but Shauna said I could use her high heels. They were a bit big but I stuffed them to the toes with newspaper. I asked Mum should I wear make- up, and she said I could try a bit of blusher and some light eye shadow. I wanted just lipstick, but went along with what she suggested. Mum gave me her make- up bag and I went into the bathroom to make myself look beautiful. I had watched Shauna and Trina do it a thousand times so it can't be difficult.

On went the eye shadow - a wee bit heavy so I'll counteract that with more blusher and lippy, but my cheeks were now glowing like a China doll. In about fifteen minutes I emerged from the toilet and Mum did well to hold in her laughter:

"Wow, that's eh lovely Billy!"

Shauna was a bit less tactful; "Who done your make- up Billy, Stevie Wonder?"

I was a bit annoyed but I knew they had my best interests at heart:

"If I look stupid the tell me," I asked.

"I'd use a bit less blusher you look like Santa's helper," said Shauna, "C'mon and I'll fix it for you." After another ten minutes my slap was removed and a new coat put on, proving less is more.

"Have you any perfume on ya?" asked Shauna.

"I haven't even got any perfume; maybe I could use a drop of yours?" I suggested. Shauna laughed: "What's with getting so dolled up tonight? Is there a man on the go?"

I went a bit red, "I'm going on a blind date," I said. Shauna roared with laughter,

"A blind date, that'll be good. Who fixed you up then?"

I told her about Claire and Colly and the set up they had, and that they had suggested they may have the ideal partner for me.

"Who are you expecting then somebody tall, dark and handsome, somebody with their own paper round?" Shauna laughed again, "What did Mum say?" she asked.

"She doesn't know and don't tell her, I'm embarrassed enough about it!"

Shauna just nodded; "Fair enough, I don't want to know the gory details anyway."

It was about 7:20pm when Claire called for me and off we went to the disco. Claire looked surprisingly well, although I doubt there was much need for the glittering headband and glitter on her cheek bones. When we got there I asked Claire about dancing as I'd never been here before, "Just follow my lead, do what I do and you'll be alright," she said.

I figured that can't be difficult. We paid our pound each in and put our coats in the cloakroom. The music was very loud and there were a lot of people in the disco. The DJ was wearing a silver T- shirt and dark glasses, though it was dark already. He stood behind two record players and had wooden boxes with lights flashing. I knew some of the songs but just walked around behind Claire. Suddenly on came Wham! and Claire bolted for he dance floor. I followed, and before I knew it there I was in the middle of the floor. In my head was 'just do what Claire does.' I watched closely. Claire threw her head back and then bent over, nearly touching her toes; when she came back up she was pulling a face- I thought she was hurt but then she started shouting; "Bad boys stick together Woo Hoo!"

She started waving her arms around her head and sticking her bum out at the back. I tried to do the same but it looked like I was having a fit of some sort. I was happy when the song was over and Claire said, "Let's get a coke and see who is about."

Again I followed in pursuit and got a drink. We were sitting near the toilets when Colly appeared. He was dressed in a black shirt and black trousers with a leather jacket on that was at least a size too big; "How's it going Claire?"

Claire was all gooey eyed. "Well Colly, did you get Billy a date?"

He shrugged his shoulders, "I brought a mate along but I don't know if he'll fancy her or not."

I butted in, "Hello, I am here like, I mightn't like him?"

Colly disappeared again and Claire and I went into the toilets.

"Billy you wait in here and I'll go and get your blind date, when he's outside I'll come and get you."

I was nervous but I agreed. Claire was back in no time and the moment had arrived.

"Are you ready Billy? Let's go and meet your Mr. Wonderful!"

I fixed my clothes and hair and walked out. There he was, standing there with a jazzy T shirt and black army trousers, a studded bracelet on one wrist and a watch on the other, boxer boots and his hair like the boy from Kagagoogoo. I couldn't believe my eyes. Claire said, "So Billy what do you think, Yes or No?"

I said, "Eh definitely not, no way on this earth, thank you!"

Claire was lost for words, "What you mean No, what's wrong with him?"

I went back into the toilet and Claire followed. "What's up Billy? Didn't you like him?"

I looked at Claire, "That's Barry," I said.

"Oh you know him already, is that it?" Claire asked.

"Know him? He's my cousin!"

I wished the ground would swallow me up, but I had to go back out into the disco. When we went back out Colly and Barry were talking, I just went straight past and away down the back. Claire came down with Colly in toe;

"Imagine that eh Billy, what a small world. Your cousin is very nice, by the way, he's getting a mountain bike for his birthday and he has a Hi-Fi."

I just wanted to go home. "He's a geek, a total dweeb, his parents get him everything, I'm going home!"

The disco wasn't over for another hour yet so I just walked around till it was over, avoiding Barry like crazy and vowing I'd never look at boys again. I got home and Mum was waiting up;

"Well Billy, did you get a boy tonight?"

I thought she's starting to sound like Nana.

"Nah no boys, just music and a mineral, I've got change from the £2 you gave me."

Mum laughed, "That's our Billy she'll not spend much money!"

I went to my room; "I'm wrecked and going on to bed," I said, "See you in the morning. Are you going up to Nana's tomorrow?" Mum asked;

"Aye maybe" was the response.

After living down the grief from Claire about Barry we finally got back to normality as our summer holidays got into full swing. We would meet up in the mornings and go down by Green water, there was always a few of us. Claire, Me, Claire's cousins Denise and Finnoula, they were twins, Colly, Mickey and Niamh came over some days and the odd time Paula, Claire's wee sister would come along but very rarely. It was a nice summers evening when my Mum came belting down by the river; "Billy! Billy C'mon quickly!" she was very distressed.

"What's wrong Mum?" I asked her, but she just kept running ahead.

"We have to get to the Hospital and there's no bus for another 20 minutes!" Mum shouted.

"My Dad could drive you Mrs Corke," said Claire, "I'll ask him now."

We got up by the Mill Hill and Claire's house. Mr Doherty came out, "Hop in there and I'll run you up to the Hospital, it'll only take five minutes, is everything ok?"

My Mum was in a right tizzy, "I hope we're not too late, this is wile decent of you!"

We all jumped into Mr Doherty's Volkswagen Beetle and headed for Southside General Hospital, just the other side of Rosnarene. Mum and Mr Doherty were talking and I tried to pick up what I could but just got mum saying; "I only got the word a half hour ago and I've rang the other family members."

I had all sorts going through my head by the time we got to the hospital. The car had barely stopped when Mum was out like a bullet and into the building. I could barely keep up, she was throwing open doors and ploughing on, she obviously knew where she was going. Finally we came to a nurse sitting at a desk. Mum and her chatted while I got my breath back, "You go and have a sit down with the nurse Billy, and I'll be back in a minute."

Mum went through more double doors and out of sight. "Do you want a colouring book or a jigsaw?" the Nurse asked.

"Nah I'm grand thanks, I'll just sit and wait," I replied. About half our later Mum came back out in floods of tears. I was scared;

"What is it Mum?" Mum sat down.

"It's a girl, a baby girl, and she's the double of her Mummy!"

I had worked out by now that Trina must have had her baby. Pauric came out in a Green surgeon's gown and his face was the same colour;

"You're an Auntie now Sarah and I am a Daddy!" he looked very pleased and turned to Mum.

"Isn't she lovely, she's just a mini Catriona?"

Not long after that Dad arrived with Shauna who had been over at Nicky's, and then we got to see Mother and baby. Trina looked a bit rough, Mum said;

"If you ever tried pushing a melon through a tennis racket then you know why she looks wrecked!"

I smiled and nodded not having a clue what that meant. At the foot of the bed was a little glass case and among the blankets were two big brown eyes and a jet black head of hair. Trina's baby was gorgeous; I was admiring her closely when: "Waaaaaaaaa!!!!" she started balling.

"I didn't touch her; I was just looking at her and she....!"

Mum interrupted; "It's ok Billy, she's maybe due a feed or needs winded."

She lifted the baby out. I have had bigger dolls than Trina's baby. They gave her a tiny bottle and then the Nurse came and took her down to the nursery and we left to let Trina get some rest herself. I couldn't wait to get home and tell everyone I was an Auntie. Mum was proud to be a Granny at 45, but Dad still wasn't sold on the idea of being called Granddad. Once home Mum was on the phone to Nana but she had to ring back as Crossroads was on. Dad rang Uncle Eamon and they said they would call and see Trina when Cassie got back from town, then they might call here. I made myself scarce and went up to Claire's to tell them the good news. I stayed up there till almost bedtime before going home but the in laws hadn't called anyway. After a few days Trina and the baby were out and we went up to Nana's.

"Bring her in till I get a look at her!" said Nana as we arrived at her flat. Trina unwrapped the tiny baby and Nana stared;

"She's dark isn't she, and she's a bit of a bruiser, what weight was she?"

Trina replied, "8 lb 6 oz."

Nana scratched her head; "I can't mind what weight your Mother was but she was a big 'un!"

Trina leaned over, "Do you want to hold her Nana?"

Nana was like a child on Christmas morning, "Aye surely, give her to me, Sarah go next door and tell Mary to come in to see the baby. Don't go to Winnie's because she has a cough and you don't want her spluttering her germs over this wee one."

I did as instructed and although it took Mary awhile to answer the door she too arrived in Nana's small living room. "She's a lovely wee thing isn't she?" said Mary, "She's like her Mummy," she continued.

"It's too early to tell yet, their features don't develop for a couple of weeks, they change so quickly," Nana said.

"What are you going to call her?" asked Mary.

"Well we thought about singers names like Whitney or Madonna or maybe even Ciara?" Trina replied.

"That's nice singers' names eh? I would go for Vera after Vera Lynne, I don't know them other ones, she used to be my favourite when she sang," Nana butted in. "Ciara not Vera, Mary, Ciara. You'll have to excuse Mary she's a bit deaf. I'm just telling them you're a bit, och never mind!" said Nana, as Mary cupped her hand to her ear and squinted.

"Why don't you call her after your Mother or his Mother, what's Paurics Mum called?" Nana enquired.

"She's dead Nana" said Trina.

"I know that, I'm not stupid but she still had a name when she was living didn't she?"

Trina smiled, "Yeah she was called Gertrude, when she was knocking about." Nana studied,

"What? You couldn't call the crater that, what are your other choices again?"

Trina was about to go through the list again when Sister Anne came in;

"Hello, the door was open I was just passing, oh a new baby. Congratulations!" she said.

"It's not mine," laughed Nana.

"Your days of having a baby are over a long time ago," said Hairy Mary with a laugh.

"Is she christened yet or what's her name?" asked Sister Anne.

"No the christening is on Sunday week after last mass and then we'll have a wee do back at Mums, so keep your diaries free that day," said Trina. At first I thought great, a party at our house and everybody will be there, and on second thoughts so will Uncle Eamon and Cassie, but more so Baz.

Chapter 6

The Sunday of the christening arrived and we all went to the chapel. Mum, Dad and I got a lift with Trina and Pauric, while Nana, Mary and Winnie all came in a taxi. Uncle Eamon had his own car with Cassie planked in the front and the dreaded Baz in the back. Paurics family were there too, well his 2 brothers and Dad anyway, and some Auntie who I'd never seen apart from the wedding day. Shauna had got a lift with Nicky's' parents who were at the last mass, and so the ceremony could begin. Fr Taggart was the man in charge as usual and everything went great.

The godparents, our Shauna and Paurics brother Darren did the honours of taking vows for the baby, and in under an hour, Whitney Agnes Casey was on her way back to our house for the party. Mum had been up since the crack of dawn making sandwiches and cleaning cups, there was apple tarts and homemade scones with jam, Dad had stocked up on wine and tins of beer and there were 2 big flans with fresh cream and fruit. Whitney was fast sleep when we got back and was put upstairs to get some peace and quiet, while the adults tucked into the buffet.

"Tea, Tea, Tea?" asked Mum while pointing at Nana and her mates. They all nodded in approval, "Can I have juice and can Claire come down for a while Mum?" I asked.

"Aye surely go and call for the wee girl sure she might as well join the crack."

Mum started to make tea and pour juice and I went for Claire. As it was a Sunday she already had her good clothes on so we were back in a flash. Dad handed out tins of beer to the men who had all gathered in one side of the kitchen, there was Nicky who Nana thought was permanently ill, Pauric and his Dad, James his brother and Darren the Godfather, he was a rare one. Big red cheeks and bright, ginger bushy hair. He laughed loudly and clapped his hands a lot. Nana said the first time he came in she thought his head was on fire, oh and that he stinks of cow muck.

"Where there's muck there's money eh Darren?" Nana would shout at him and he'd say,

"By Jasus you're right there!" Then he'd spit on his hands and laugh again. The three old ladies had taken up residency on the sofa, while Trina and Shauna had grabbed the arm chairs; Mum was in an out of the kitchen so Claire and I sat on the stairs.

"There are Eamon and Cassie Mum!" shouted Trina.

"Oh I'd forgotten about them, where did they go after the chapel anyway?" asked Mum.

"They had to go to the shop and get painkillers for the lad," explained Dad.

They came in and I wondered how long it would be before mouthy Baz would mention the blind date fiasco and I'd be disgraced, but he came in and went straight into the living room without a word. Claire said; "What's up with him?"

I didn't have an answer so just shrugged. Cassie was soon into the scones and tea while Eamon couldn't enjoy a beer as he thinks he has a bladder problem.

"Does it sting like mad when you piss?" asked the flame haired Darren.

"No just a bit uncomfortable," was Eamon's reply.

"It stings when I pee," said Winnie, "I got the cold in my kidneys and it's very unpleasant, it's like trying to pass glass sometimes."

Winnie sighed. Mary piped up; "You should thank you lucky stars, I haven't been able to go since Thursday, I'm bound up and I've tried everything and nothing will shift me."

Nana was in like a bullet, "Thanks for sharing your bowel movements with us all, the clinic will be open soon for back pain, arthritis, coughs, sneezes and feet. In grown toe nails, bunions and corns!" The place erupted in laughter, Nana was good at taking the spotlight. Claire and I sat and had a mini feast in the hallway with juice and food then Baz appeared.

"Howsss the girlsss?" he asked.

"Dead on Barry, what's the crack with you, any more blind dates?" Claire joked and I poked her in the side.

"Blind datesss, I have better sings to do than waste my time on silly blind dates with kidsss."

I was a bit angry; "What do you mean kids, granddad what age are you?" I said sharply.

"Chill Billy you're not my type even if you weren't my cousin, I'm sooting a bit higher!"

Claire butted in; "Why are you talking funny, is there something in your mouth?"

Baz put his hand over his mouth, "Ssshut up!" At that his Mum Cassie came into the hall:

"Barry love did you take the tablets before you eat anything?"

She then saw us on he stairs, "Hi ya girls I suppose he's been telling you about near been killed?" "Ssssussh Ma will ya!!"

I pretended to be concerned; "Nah Auntie Cassie what happened?" Cassie leaned on the banister;

"Eamon got him a new mountain bike and he was out at our place riding around, he was probably showing off when he went down McErleans hill to the junction and didn't McErleans old mongrel run out barking at his heels and he swerved, hit the footpath and went over the handlebars and knock two teeth out in the front, show them," she said.

"Why do you have to tell everything eh?"

Baz had his head down frowning at his Mother story.

"Ooops I doubt I've spoiled a bigger story girls," she laughed and went into the kitchen again.

"Is it very sssore Bazzz; would you like an sssucky sssweet?" Claire teased.

"Very funny Sponge face," he said.

"What, what's sponge face?" Claire asked.

"That's what Colly Thompson calls you. He said you kissed him once and it was like a car wash all slobbers and spit."

Barry's reply sounded worse through the gap of the missing teeth. Claire was furious.

"You tell Thompson you'll not be the only one with teeth missing when I get him!"

I said; "Baz why don't you grow up and shut up, look what you've started now!" He wiped his lips, "Sshe started on me, so you shut up Billy bowl head!"

I stood up to make my comeback but Mum appeared; "Everything ok out here?"

Baz walked in past her, "Aye everything's fine if you keep toothless in the other room, C'mon Claire," I said grabbing my coat and going out the front door.

Claire was a bit upset at what Barry had said and we hadn't gone far when Mickey Thompson came into view.

"Here c'mon here I want you, where's your Colin at?" Claire asked him.

"Colin is down at the house helping me Dad cut the hedge; if you hurry down they might take a bit of that belly off you." Mickey's reply was as nasty as ever.

"Why don't you just answer the question and stop being so nasty to her?" I said.

"Shut your mouth pinhead and go suck the face off your cousin," he came back. Claire and I were both very angry now; "You've gone too far this time," Claire said as she started towards him. I was running behind.

"Ha look at the state of you. Help! I'm being chased by the number 10, a fatty and a skinny!"

Mickey roared as he ran for home, he was small but he was quick. Up past the Mill Hill we weren't gaining much, round the next corner we expected Mickey to be out of sight but instead he was stretched out on the pavement. He had rounded the corner and stood on wee Paula's roller skates outside the gate; the feet had left him and he was in a heap.

"I think I've broken my left arm!" he sobbed.

"That's ok, I'll lift you by the other one," Claire said pulling him off the ground. The knee was ripped in his Sunday trousers and the jumper was covered in dirt.

"We'll walk you home in case you fall again," Claire sniggered as she pushed him ahead of us down the lane to his house. When we got there Colly was putting bushes into a coal bag for dumping, while his Dad was up a step ladder trimming the hedge.

"I brought you a present," Claire said. Colly replied:

"Hi ya, are you alright? I thought you were away to bowlheads for the big do?"

I appeared around the hedge; "Oh hello Billy I didn't see you there, is the party over?" he continued. I didn't get to say anything before Claire started:

"Your wee brother fell and hurt his arm, he's put the knee out of his trousers too and I bet your Ma will warm his ears, he deserves all he gets for being so cheeky!"

I think he was about to agree when she continued; "You're in different trouble though. Barry Corke said you called me Sponge face, he said that you told everybody I kissed you and it was like going through the car wash? Well did you say that?"

Colin stuttered, "I didn't mean it in a bad way like, it's just how it came out. We were talking about the

88

disco on the bus one day and I said kissing you was like kissing a wet sponge."

Claire was boiling up; "Is that supposed to make it better?" she raised her voice much louder, "Was that the disco you tried to smoke a cigarette with Emmet Bradley, do you remember you were sick and vomited on your Jam T shirt, you had to get chewing gum off me on the road home because your breath was stinking of smoke and you didn't want your parents to know?"

At that Colin's Dad appeared round the hedge, "You have a bit of explaining to do!" he said looking at Colin, "What happened to you?" he asked turning to Mickey.

"I was going up to the park, minding my own business when these two set upon me, first the skinny one started calling me names then the bigger one said that she'd hold me down and sit on me 'till I couldn't breathe!"

Mickey was very believable though I don't think his Dad bought the story.

"Why did they bring you home then?" he asked. Mickey replied:

"I told them if they didn't hurt me then I'd give them money from my piggy bank and so I came home to get it."

Mr Thompson asked him; "How did you tear your trousers?"

Mickey's response was quick, "I fell off the roundabout." His Father said;

"But these two girls set upon you before you got to the park you said?"

There was a silence before Mr Thompson said; "I know two lads who are in quite a bit of trouble, I suggest you get in the house and God knows what the punishment will be when your Mum hears about this." Claire said;

"Mickey was the one doing the name calling and he fell over my wee sisters' skates when running away and Colin told us he was allowed fags and you knew he tried smoking. I hope I haven't got them in trouble?"

Mr Thompson bit his lip; "At least someone is telling the truth around here, don't worry girls you'll get no more bother from these pair!" He turned and ushered the sorry pair into the house with Mickey still protesting his innocence. Claire nudged me;

"C'mon Billy," and we walked away, very content that we had exacted revenge on the evil Thompson twins.

Claire went home and I headed back into the Grange. I could hear the noise coming from our house before I even got in, when I opened the door Hairy Mary and Pauric were singing "Summer Nights" in the front room with Winnie, Darren and Dad accompanying them. Mum and Shauna were washing up the dishes, and Cassie was drying. James, Nicky, Eamon and toothless Barry were trying to watch some match on the telly, while Paurics Dad had taken Trina over to her house for a change of clothes for Whitney.

"Your back Sarah, I've left you a bit of cake there on the side board," said Mum.

"Cheers Mum I love cake, Where's Nana?" I asked.

"She was a bit tired and tiddly so she's away up for a lie down, she'll be down in a bit," Mum said. I took my cake and went up to see how Whitney was getting on but when I got to my room Nana was there talking to the baby.

"You're probably wondering what the whole fuss is about eh?" she said to the baby. "I'm your Nana, nah hold on I'm your great Nana, you're looking up at me and thinking, who the hell is that with the wrinkly face? At least the two of us look the same when we smile!" Nana laughed, "You're a lucky girl, you know. Aye they're a good lot the Corkes and O Hares. Your Mummy and Daddy will see you want for nothing and if they do then you call your Nana and I will be here. Anyway you go to sleep now and I'll go back down before they think I've died up here, God Bless wee love," Nana giggled "Thank your lucky stars you're not called Gertrude after your Nana Casey."

Nana stood up and a little gas escaped, she turned, "Oooops, better out than in eh Sarah, I was checking in on the child there she is grand.

"Nana walked out of the room and headed for the party downstairs, I went to bed thinking to myself she's a good old girl.

It was no time at all to Mum and I were back in Brendan Walsh's drapery shop, but there was no need for a full uniform this time just a new blouse and Green tights, and a week later I was waiting on the bus with Claire. She hadn't made up with Colly and he hadn't forgiven her for getting him in trouble. Mickey was doing his final year at the primary so I hadn't seen much of him since the day he fell over the skates. Back in school I was able to look at the scared faces of the first years and think I'm a regular here now. Sister Bridget was taking the new ones as she had with us 12 months ago and we had moved onto Sister Theresa, she was a different kettle of fish. Sister Theresa was very strict, no jewellery, no make up, no matter how little, skirts well below the knee, punctuality was vital and the prayers and respect were the most important thing in the world. Niamh was terrified of her and Madonna wasn't far behind. I got to say I wasn't that fond of her either but kept my head down and got on with my work. Nana and her two companions were getting on great in the sheltered housing and when her bingo pal Elsa moved into the empty flat she had all her mates around her. I would call in about twice a week and had some good laughs with the four of them; they all would go to Nana's and play cards. It was a Wednesday afternoon when I called and the cards were in full swing. I pressed the buzzer and Nana said, "Hello who's that?"

I replied, "Just me Nana, Billy." A few seconds later the buzzer went again and I could go in. The living room was full with the four old ladies sitting around a coffee table, they all had little piles of silver coins stacked in front of them and had their best poker faces on. I'm not sure what the stakes were but it meant a lot to them.

"A Jack to you Mary," said Winnie. Mary checked her hand and tutted;

"No good to me." She picked a card off the deck in the middle pulling it up close to her chest before looking at it. "Nah no good!" She threw a 6 of diamonds.

"That's rummy!" shouted Elsa, laying all her cards on the table and starting to scoop up the coins. "My God Mary that's the third hand you've threw away the day," said Nana, "You're not watching and you're costing me a fortune!"

Elsa chimed in, "Och give over Aggie, you think you'd lost a hundred pound to hear you."

Elsa was stacking the coins in a pile. "Sarah, make a wee cup of tea like a good child, there's a packet of biscuits in the press."

I asked was everybody having tea and got three yes's and a grunt from Mary whom I think was huffing after Nana had shouted at her. I went into the kitchen and put out the cups and boiled the kettle, I went to get milk from the fridge but when I opened the door there was a mouse trap in the fridge. I called Nana and she came into the kitchen; "What's that Nana?" I said pointing to the trap, "It's a thing for catching mice Sarah," she said looking at me with her eyebrows raised, "Have you never seen one of them before?" she asked.

"Eh yeah I know what it is, but what's it doing in the fridge?" Nana started to explain;

"A couple of nights ago I was in my bed when I heard a scratching noise and a first I thought it was Sheba, but then I remembered I had put her out before going to bed. So I pressed me button and Charlie come round and had a look. He found a wee hole behind the cooker and said I must have a mouse. Well with Mary next door I told her the mouse is able to go back and forward from her house to mine through the hole behind the cooker, but she said no because she doesn't have a hole behind her cooker, she has a hole behind her fridge though."

I was going to interrupt and explain that it's probably the same hole but Nana went on, "So the next morning Mary and me went into town and got these traps, and the fella in the shop said the wee devils are after food. That's were I keep the cheese so I put it in there and he'll soon be caught now, isn't that right?"

Nana looked pleased with herself, and I was going to explain that the mouse couldn't open the fridge but the front door buzzer went and Nana dashed for the living room. I followed and there were Winnie and Elsa gathering up the cards and money like crazy, Nana joined them;

"Hurry up before they look through the window!"

They stuffed the cards into the drawer and grabbed a seat. Mary said, "What's happening, are you finished playing?" she still had her cards in her hand. Nana shouts;

"Sarah, take them cards off Mary and put them in the kitchen before whoever that is at he door comes in!"

I did what Nana said, as the door buzzed again;

"Hello, who's that?" asks Nana.

"It's Sister Bridget, I'm going into town does anybody want anything?" Nana quickly replied;

"No thank you Sister we're all grand."

Sister Bridget said; "If you're sure then I'll pop in on my way back for a wee chat."

Sister Bridget left and Nana said; "That was a close one, they don't like gambling, the Sisters. Elsa, I thought you were keeping dick?"

Elsa was busy putting the coins into her purse, "I was collecting my winnings, sure they're none the wiser!" she laughed. I didn't know what to think, the four of them were as bad as each other, like teenagers breaking the rules. They were having a giggle about getting away with it when Mary said, "Is the game over or will somebody tell me what's happening?"

Winnie explained loudly that Sister Bridget was at the door, and Mary finally got the message and went home to her own flat taking the other two with her. I helped Nana take the trap out of the fridge and headed for home myself. The house was empty with Mum away over to Trina's to see the baby. That was the plan on a Wednesday, she had the cleaning job Tuesday and Thursday so she called to see Whitney on the day off in between. I was at the kitchen table when the phone rang, I picked it up and was gobsmacked to hear Beth on the other side:

"Is that Billy?" she asked.

"Aye, it's me, is that Beth?" was my reply.

"Yeah it's Beth, I didn't think you'd recognise me or if you even had the same number, how are you all keeping, and any crack with you?"

I had so much to tell her but was still a little confused as to why she had rang.

"Well my Nana has moved up to St Frances', that's were I go to school. I got friends called Claire, Niamh and Madonna. Eh, our Trina got married and has a wee girl called Whitney, Shauna is in the Uni, my Nana has got new friends too called Winnie, Hairy Mary and Elsa, who also live in the sheltered housing..."

I was rattling off as much as I could remember since I had last seen Beth almost three years ago. "How's things with you Beth, what you been up to then, How's your Mum?"

I was so excited to hear from Beth I was bombarding her with questions.

"Kiltamnagh is alright, when you get used to it and my Mum is grand. She just lost her job in the school kitchen. She was helping out there but they're cutting back on anybody who doesn't have qualifications. I go to the school as well, it's called Kiltamnagh High but it's nothing special like. Anyway I'll tell you more when I see you!"

I didn't think I heard her right; "When you see me?" I asked in expectation.

"Yeah we're coming down to the Grange for Christmas, Mum has had letters and cards not to mention a stack of calls from my Granny asking to see me, and although at the start Mum said a straight No, she thinks that it's not Granny's' fault that her and my Dad split up, so she said we would go down over the holidays."

I couldn't believe it Beth was coming to the Grange. "Do you know what date? How long you staying for?

And where does your Nana live?" The questions keep coming from me.

"We're arriving on 23rd of December and staying till the new year, just about a week or so," Beth continued, "My Granny lives just outside the town a bit between Finagate and Rosnarene, do you know it?" she asked.

"Aye I've got a friend called Madonna who lives in Finagate, it's not that far from the Grange just a bus trip really," I said.

"Well I'd better go. Mum said I could call and let you know; she says tell your Mum she'll call when we get down there, its great chatting to you Billy and I'll see you soon, Bye!" Beth concluded.

"See ya soon Beth, Bye!"

I was over the moon and couldn't wait to tell Mum. The fact that Beth hadn't kept in touch was a distant memory and all was forgiven. Mum got home and I was straight in with the news;

"Mum when I got home today I got a phone call from Beth, Beth Mackle. You'll never believe this, her and her Mummy are coming down here for Christmas holidays, they're staying with her Granny in Finagate for a week!" Mums face was a picture;

"That's great news, I haven't seen them in years, that's really good news. I'm looking forward to that now!" she said.

Over the next couple of months I told everyone about my best mate Beth coming for the holidays. I made a few trips to Madonna's house in Finagate and checked out where Mrs Mackle lived, she was a nice lady who had a wee white washed cottage between

Finagate and Rosnarene town. Madonna knew her quite well as she did a paper round there and said she always gave a bit extra for herself. On the bus I told Claire about Beth and how we were the best friends ever until she had to move away but now she is coming for the holidays and I was so happy. I even told the Nuns at the convent about Beth's pending arrival and they were pleased for me though I don't think it was that big a deal to them. When I told Nana she said, "Is that the wee lassie that headed off bag and baggage a few months ago after the Mother and Father couldn't agree?"

I explained that it was nearly three years from they went but Nana didn't understand, she had troubles of her own as she had lost her walking stick and was convinced that Sheba had took it and buried it in the garden.

Chapter 7

Needless to say the time flew in to Christmas, and as predicted on December 23rd Beth and her Mum arrived in Rosnarene bus station and made their way to Garland Cottage where they would be staying for the next eight days. I let them settle in the first night and on Christmas Eve they came down to the Grange. Our house was packed as it always was on Christmas Eve with Trina and Pauric and wee Whitney (who was 5 months old now) calling in with presents. Eamon, Cassie and Barry were there because they didn't go anywhere on Christmas Day as Eamon and Cassie would be sampling all the sherry and wine that was on the go and Baz was getting an Atari video game thingy for to play games on the telly. Shauna was home for the holidays too, so it was like a mad house when Beth and her Mum Teresa arrived.

"Nothing changes eh, the Corke house is always full," said Beth's Mum as she came in the door, then in came Beth and I saw her for the first time since I was nine;

"Hi Billy, how are you?" she asked, but I just ran over and hugged her. She had certainly got a lot bigger in the two and a bit year away. My Mum was hugging her Mum, and there were a few tears. They had brought us some presents, they were wrapped up but I don't think anybody cared much about presents.

"You're down for the holidays Teresa?" Mum asked.

"Aye, I thought it only fair to take Beth down to see his Ma, after all it wasn't her fault we couldn't sort things, and God knows she has asked me enough times. She's not the worst of them you know, and she'd never miss her birthday without a card and a few pound in it, so I decided we'd come down for a few days. You're looking well Imelda, how's Tommy and you coping with being Grandparents?" Beth's Mum continued, "Congratulations Trina on your new arrival and this must be the lucky man" she said shaking Paurics hand. Mum did the formal introductions to the rest of the clan who didn't know who Beth and Teresa were, while Beth and I went for a walk.

Beth had changed a lot. She was taller and had lost her boyish short hair, and as Nana would say she filled out her top better now. We walked along and I was asking her a million questions as usual when we arrived at the park. It was pretty cold so we snuggled together on the roundabout to keep warm while we shared stories of our past.

"Hi ya Sarah, I called down at your house but your Ma said you were away out, I thought you might be here?" It was Claire;

"Oh hi ya Claire, this is my friend Beth I was telling you about, you remember the girl from Kiltamnagh that used to live here, Beth this is Claire another friend of mine she goes on the same bus as me to school."

The two girls exchanged greetings and we started chatting. After a while the Thompsons came along and Mickey was as mouthy as ever.

"There's pin head and motor mouth, and they have picked a third stray from somewhere, who are you then?"

Beth looked at him; "Who are you; you're a nosey wee gob?"

Claire joined in; "That's the Thompsons, they don't get out much, they have been grounded for months."

Mickey kept on; "Aye sponge face there tells tales, and pinhead kissed her cousin at the disco the sicko, but we don't know you and by the look of you you're not related to these animals"

Beth smiled, "You're a sweet talker for such a wee lad, do you do all the taking in your house? You'd need to give your mouth a rest."

Mickey came straight back, "That's my brother Colin, he doesn't talk to these two because they got him into bother with my ol' boy over the summer, they got me into trouble too there mouthy cows, especially the fat one!"

He stepped back a bit and went on; "Who are you? You're not from round here?"

Claire said, "Shove off and mind your own business, go and find somebody else to bug would you?" she sniggered, "Did your Mummy not tell you about calling people names?"

Colin spoke up, "C'mon Mickey there's no point starting hassle with them lot, come on I'm heading home."

Colly walked towards the gates, "Merry Christmas!" said Claire in a sarcastic tone but Colin just walked on. Mickey shouted:

"There'll not be many spare mince pies in your house anyway!" The boys disappeared out of sight as Claire told Beth the story of how she got them both in trouble over the summer. Beth wasn't impressed and said, "That was a bit childish wasn't it, telling their Dad on them; where I live you don't tell tales."

Claire was taken by surprise, as I was, and left saying, "I'll give you a shout tomorrow Sarah with your Christmas present."

I replied, "Aye I'll call you for after dinner, I hope Santa comes!"

It was starting to get late, so Beth and I made tracks for my house and then she had to go to her Granny's' cottage.

"I'll see you when we're coming up to the Grange again Billy ok?" Beth said as she was leaving.

"Aye let me know or maybe I could call out to your Nanas house?"

Beth and her Mum hopped in the taxi and off they went. I went to bed early, well it was Christmas tomorrow.

Christmas morning and I was opening my presents. There was an envelope from Madonna with a voucher to the cinema, I got gloves and a scarf from Nana and I got a musical jewellery box from Beth and Teresa. Mum and Dad had got me new clothes, and Trina and Pauric had got me a gift token for the music store, and surprise, surprise Shauna had got me a brush and mirror set. I got my friends all the same thing, beaded necklaces with their names spelled out on cubes with a letter on each. I got Dad aftershave and Mum chocolates, I got Whitney a set of bibs with; "My First Christmas" on them. I got Shauna a sparkly belt and I got Nana a new mug with 'My Favourite Nan' written on it. We all went to Christmas day mass and afterwards had our big Turkey dinner with crackers and all the trimmings, it was great. Nana had a wee sherry and looked a picture in her paper hat, "What secret agent comes around at Christmas time?" she asked.

"Don't know Nana," I replied.

"Mince Spy!" she said.

We were all laughing when Nana said, "I don't get that, does anybody get that, who is Mince Spy? I never heard of him or her are they like Colombo?"

Mum took a phone call and was very smiley when she came in. "Sarah we've been invited over to Garland Cottage for the afternoon when your Dad goes to the pub and Nana goes up home."

I was up for that, and about 2:30ish we got a lift into town with Paurics brother Darren and walked the short distance out to the Cottage. Once inside I gave Beth her present and she said, "I'll wear it with this one." She showed me the necklace I had brought her from Kilrushden after our trip there in 1980. The Mums and Mrs Mackle senior sat down to tea and Christmas cake while Beth and I went over to Finagate and called at Madonna's. Again I was delivering my present and thanked her for mine.

"What did she get you?" asked Beth as we walked along.

"A voucher for the cinema, I can go whenever I want to."

Madonna said, "Maybe we could go over the holidays, there's bound to be something good on, I'll ask my Dad?"

Beth asked, "How does your Dad know what's on at the cinema, does he own the place?"

Madonna looked up to the sky, "Nah he doesn't own it, he works there though doing the projector." I already knew that because Madonna had said one time at school when we had a class about families and occupations. Beth was questioning her again; "Is that where you got the free vouchers from then?"

Madonna's face went red, "No I got the voucher because I thought Billy would like to go to the pictures sometime, that's all," she explained."Doesn't matter where I got the vouchers from does it?"

Beth laughed, "Not much of a gift is it, free vouchers off your Dad!"

Madonna was very embarrassed and said, "I have to go home now Billy, we're going away, I'll see you later."

Before I could say anything Madonna was away down the road home. I felt awful;

"You shouldn't have said that Beth, it's the thought that counts when someone gives you a present, not the value or where it came from, I think you hurt Madonna's feelings?"

Beth shrugged her shoulders, "She'll get over it, I only asked her a question, c'mon I'm freezing!" We went back down to the cottage and played some board games and watched Christmas Day Top of the Pops, before Mum and I had to go home after 6:00pm. When we got back Dad had returned from the pub and was a little worse for the drink,

"There was a young girl here for you Billy, said she had called three times but there was no-one in?" I just remembered Claire and I were to meet up after dinner and exchange presents. Mum said it was too late to go up to the Mill Hill now and besides it was dark outside so leave it till tomorrow. I felt awful again and Boxing Day morning I was up and away up to Claire's first thing. Claire came out and I said, "I brought your present up, I hope you like it?" Claire didn't say anything but went back inside and came back with a gift wrapped up.

"Here you go Billy, Happy Boxing day," she said with a frown.

"Is everything ok Claire?" I asked.

"Well Billy, no actually, we had made plans to meet up yesterday afternoon, exchange presents and spend Christmas Day doing stuff, instead I spent my Christmas walking up and down to your house like Billy no mates while you went swanking off with your mates."

I tried to interrupt and explain but Claire said, "Forget it Billy, thank you for the present I got to go." She went back into her house and closed the door. When I got back home Beth and her Mum were there,

Mum had invited them to our place because we had went to them on Christmas Day. I had planned to go to Niamhs house with Claire but I guessed that wasn't going to happen now. Mum suggested Beth and I go to the matinee at the cinema and use up my voucher and she would pay for Beth, and after much persuading we got the bus into Rosnarene and arrived at the cinema. We had got in the queue and got our tickets when I saw Niamh,

"Hey Niamh, how's it going, I didn't know you were going to the flicks today?"

Niamh said, "Well I wasn't going to sit in the house and wait on you calling, I rang Claire and she said you were up at her house and then she was out with her sister Paula for a walk and saw you had visitors arriving, so Claire's meeting me and Madonna here to go to cinema."

Beth chimed in; "That other doll must have got you all free vouchers, I'm the only one paying here!" Beth pushed past us, "C'mon Billy or the good seats will be all taken!"

I asked Niamh to join us but she refused and said she was waiting for Claire and Madonna. I went on in with Beth and took our seats, though I'd much rather waited for the others. Midway through "M Mom," I went up to the ice cream man and Madonna was in the line.

"The film is very good isn't it? I said and Madonna replied;

"I suppose you enjoy it more when you get in for nothing with the free tickets I got off my Dad."

106

She got her ice cream and walked off. I had just about had enough of this and followed her back to her seats where the other two were waiting:

"What's the problem eh, have I done something that pissed you off, if so I'd like to hear it?" Claire said; "You just dumped us when the wonderful Beth came along. You forgot about me Christmas Day, you insulted Madonna's present and then you weren't even going to bother calling at Niamhs house today, so why don't you just go back down to Beth and watch the film!"

I was very cross; "I forgot about calling yesterday, a simple mistake Claire, secondly I never mocked Madonna's present and I was going to call at Niamhs after the pictures. Beth is only here for a week and your acting like jealous children!"

Niamh and Madonna sat quiet but Claire said, "Blah, Blah, Blah, what ever, tell it to somebody that cares."

I said, "Grow up Claire!" and stormed off to my seat.

"What's up with you?" asked Beth.

"Nothing, just people being stupid, that's all."

Beth said, "Never worry about them they're just being childish, they'll grow up someday."

I agreed; "You're right Beth I don't need that lot whinging on at me every time I don't jump to what they say."

Beth said, "Good for you Billy stand up for yourself!"

We watched the rest of the film and at the end I just stormed out past the other girls and went straight for the bus. When I got back home Beth told my mum all about the incident with Madonna, Niamh and Claire. Mum said:

"It's not like you Billy to fall out with them girls, you're usually as thick as thieves?" I replied;

"Well they're acting like babies."

Beth joined in, "They were, and Sarah just stood up to them."

Mum said "There's more to this than meets the eye, I'm sure you will sort yourselves out."

Mum and Beth's Mum went into the kitchen while Beth and I watched telly in the front room till they went home. The rest of the holidays were spent doing stuff. Dad had an all boys gathering on the 28th with Eamon, Baz, James, Pauric, Darren and his mate Kieran from work, plus Paurics Dad, but Shauna's boyfriend Nicky couldn't come as it was the same night Shauna and him were going to a Christmas Fayre and Disco. We were all shipped out to various places, Mum went to Trina's and I went up to spend the night in Nana's with her. When I arrived, Nana was watching an old Steptoe film and laughing away to herself;

"He's great that old boy, reminds me of your granddad God rest him, and the son looks like your Dad Tom but don't say I said that, How was your Christmas then?" she asked.

"It was great Nana, Beth was down and we went to the pictures yesterday but it ended up a disaster," I continued, "You know Claire?" I asked.

"Is that the wee heavy girl?" Nana replied.

"Aye that's her, well she had went to the pictures with Madonna and Niamh from my class and when I went up to say hello they started on me about how since Beth came I neglected them, so I told them to grow up, was I right Nana?"

Nana looked confused, "Who are Niamh and Madonna again, have I met them before cause if I have I can't place them."

I explained again but Nana shook her head, "Nah don't know them, but if they were your friends before this other doll came then she must be the problem, they might be jealous?" Nana went on, "I had only moved up here a while when I got a visit from Elsa and before I knew where I was she was here all the time, I think she's jealous of my wee flat and she's trying to get one herself. I see her about right and regular."

I interrupted; "But Nana Elsa has a flat here she lives just two doors away from you!"

Nana looked at me, "Since when?"

I sighed, "Since ages Nana, sure does she call in for the cards and that?" I asked.

"Well she could have said, the whole time we've been playing rummy and I was asking her over to have a game, and she never mentioned that she lives just beside me, what's more she has been calling with me and eating me out of house and home and I thought she was doing me a good turn by coming out to me, the crafty old devil! " Nana got up, "Wait you here child till I go and tell Mary the carry on!" I stopped her;

109

"Nana, Mary knows where Elsa lives and so does Winnie." She looked even more shocked;

"It's a conspiracy," she shuffled back in. I knew in an hour or so she'd remember the whole thing of Elsa moving in.

"Did you ever catch the mouse Nana?"

Nana plonked down in the arm chair, "What mouse?"

I thought to myself, this is going to be a long night, "The mouse that was in the kitchen? The one that was going back and forward between you and Mary's place through the hole behind the cooker?" I asked again:

"How the hell could I catch the mouse, I got a trap and put it in where the food was and when I went back it was away" Nana had the telly remote, "What time does Del Boy start at? There's a magazine under the cushion."

I hadn't even answered her about the Mouse yet. "It says Only Fools and Horses starts at half eight." She looked at me strangely, "I don't watch those old nature or wildlife programmes, what time is Del Boy on? Is it after that horses programme?" she said.

Nana was in good form tonight, though slower on the uptake than usual, and then I found out the reason why. I went into the kitchen and there sat the remains of a box of chocolates. On closer inspection I found they were a box of liquors and Nana had scoffed nearly them all, she was half drunk! When I returned to the living room there she was on her knees trying to work the video recorder that Mum and Dad had got her for

Christmas, she turned to me and with her finger up to her lips she ushered me into the kitchen.

"What's up Nana?" I asked.

"I'm going to tape the Del Boy show for later so I don't want that new machine to pick up us talking," she said.

"It only records the pictures of what's on the telly Nana, not us" I explained.

"Sure what good is that? When I watch it back tomorrow I won't know what they're saying, I'll be like Mary next door I'll have to lip read, its not much of a gadget that is it?" she said opening the kitchen door again. As we made our way back into the front room the doorbell went;

"Thank God for that, somebody who talks a bit of sense, no offence Sarah," Nana said.

"Oh aye, none taken Nana." I think I was as relieved as she was that somebody else was joining us.

After the usual exchange through the intercom system Winnie appeared in the living room, she was decked out in brown fake fur coat and matching fake fur hat.

"Where are going all dressed up?" asked Nana.

"Aren't we going to the bizarre down in the parochial centre?" Winnie replied.

"I forgot all about that, and I can't go now I've a visitor," Nana said as she nodded her head towards me.

"I could go too if that's alright with you?" I asked, and Winnie gave the approval.

"Aye get your coat and we'll all go for the night out!" Nana stood up:

"Right I'll go and put on me face and spend a penny and then we'll hit the road!"

About fifteen minutes later we were in the taxi and at the parochial centre. The annual bizarre raised money for the convent and all the shops donated prizes and once you were in you would buy tickets and the man would spin a big wheel. If your ticket number came up you would go and pick a prize. Nana and Winnie sat down along the wall on a bench;

"If we'd have been early we would have got a soft seat, I won't be sitting here long to my bum goes to sleep," Nana complained.

"Here child, go and get us a strip of tickets there," Winnie said holding out a five pound note.

"Get me a strip when you're at it and I'll get them the next time and get yourself some. The more the merrier eh?" laughed Nana.

The first couple of times the wheel went round we checked our tickets but no luck, about half an hour later came the success. Nana had bought this round of tickets and her number 83 was called out.

"Away you go there Sarah and pick a prize, and pick something I'd like and if there's nothing I like pick something that'll do somebody else as a present!"

I walked up the floor and after the ticket was examined I had a good look around, and although there were lots of items, I picked a beautiful flowery jardinière. It was really pretty but quite big so the man suggested I leave it there and collect it at the end. I returned to Winnie and Nana at the bench:

"Well what did you get?" asked Nana.

"A beautiful jardinière Nana," I replied.

"A what, a jar of what? What did she say Winnie?" Nana asked her friend.

"I don't know what she said Aggie, something to do with your hair I think?" was Winnie's interpretation.

"A Jardinière Nana, it's a pot on a stand and it's made of porcelain stuff and you keep things in it."

I tried to explain,

"Like a plant or something?" she asked.

"Aye, or other things but a plant is probably best," I agreed.

"Is there no bottles of anything or boxes of biscuits, or anything electrical like a toaster up there?" Winnie inquired.

"There is a set of them cordless phones," I said.

"Cordless phones, what the hell would us two old biddies do with a cordless telephone; I can hardly remember the number of my flat let alone a phone number."

I figured I'll just shut up and let them argue over the next prize, but there wasn't one. At the end the man who was spinning the wheel came down with the jardinière:

"Mrs O Hare? Here's your prize from earlier," he said holding out the stand and pot.

"Isn't that lovely Winnie, just what I needed for the front room, thanks very much," Nana said taking the pot.

"You're very welcome, and enjoy the rest of the holidays!" the man said as he walked away.

113

"What am I going to do with this eh? It's a blooming eyesore," said Nana, "reminds me of what we used to have under the bed years ago, saved us from going to the outside one!"

Winnie laughed and Nana joined in the joke; "You'd be making a right delivery if you could fill that!" The two of them were cackling away like two old hens.

"Sarah, take that stand to we get home for a cup of tea."

I took the stand and we headed off back to Nanas. When we got back Nana was a bit tired and went to bed, Winnie went home and I watched a bit of telly before retiring to the spare room. Next morning I was up and away home as Nana was having a bit of a sleep over. The 29th and 30th were pretty uneventful and then it was New Years Eve, and we were preparing for a party. New years was always a great night in the Grange, everybody from all around the area would gather together at the big tree in the town and at 12:00 we'd sing Auld Lang Syne and wish each other a Happy New Year. Then there would be some fireworks and then home for around 1:00. Mum, Dad, Nana, Shauna and I went good and early and got good places near the tree. Trina and Pauric decided it was too cold for Whitney so they stayed at home. Teresa and Beth arrived but her Granny decided to give it a miss this year, so Beth and I went down the shop to get sweets and a drink. In the shop we met Niamh with her brother Luke, but they just blanked us and walked on by. When we got back to the tree I saw Niamh, her brother Luke, the Thompsons, Claire and even Madonna had came down. Barry arrived with his Dad complaining about the cold, and then he too went and joined the others. Mum asked why we didn't go over but Beth said, "We weren't invited and who needs them eh Billy?"

I was always in that group, although this year the plans hadn't included me obviously so I just messed about with Beth, and when the New Year came we stood with our Mums and sang away. It was a good night, but not as good as every other year. After the fireworks we went home and next morning I got the bus into Rosnarene and walked out to Garland Cottage. When I got there Mrs Mackle was in the garden;

"Hello Mrs Mackle is Beth up yet?" I asked jokingly.

"Beth? Beth has been up for hours love, her and her Mum must be near home by now I'd say?" she replied.

"Home, you mean she's already away?" I asked.

"Aye first thing this morning, they got a taxi into the station and the early bus back to Kiltamnaght, she said it was too early to ring you but she will later on today."

I was gutted Beth had gone again and not even a word. I got the bus home and told Mum about Beth and her Mum, "Aye Teresa was saying last night they might try and get away early, it's the bank holiday so the bus service mightn't be great today," Mum explained, "Why don't you head away up to Claire's and see what she's up to?"

I remembered I had something to do in my room and just stayed there. I wasn't speaking to Claire or Madonna or Niamh and if they wanted to talk then they could come to me. Needless to say apart from Mum suggesting I go up to Claire's there was no contact or mention from the others.

The holidays were soon over and I was back at the top of the road waiting on the bus when Claire came around the corner and stood a couple of feet away.

"Had you a good Christmas and New Year?" I said trying to break the ice.

"It was fine, no thanks to you. Niamh, Madonna and I made the best of it," she said turning her back to me.

"What did you want me to do Claire, I didn't do anything deliberately, it was just a misunderstanding like. I apologise if I hurt your feelings but I didn't mean to!"

Claire turned to me and said; "You dumped on all your friends when Beth came along and now she's away home you think you'll just call on us again, well that won't work. I was your friend until Beth showed up and then I wasn't required so you know what you can do with your apology!"

I was very upset, but got the message loud and clear. The bus came and we sat in separate seats and she talked to everybody on that bus about what a great time she had with her new mates Niamh and Madonna over the holidays. I just sat alone. The only person to speak to me was Colin Thompson, which made Claire dislike me even more. He only wanted to know who Beth was. Meanwhile in school it was much the same. Madonna wouldn't sit beside me but instead swapped with the girl beside Niamh in every class. I was so on my own, in class, at break time and at dinner time, even the bus home was awful. After a few days of the silent treatment I was asked to go to Sister Bridget's class as she wanted to see me;

"What's the story with you and the others Sarah?" she asked, and I told her how over the holidays things had unintentionally went sour between us. I told her about Beth and she explained;

"The girls are maybe a little jealous that you spent so much time with this Beth girl and not with them, they thought they meant more to you," I interrupted;

"They do Sister, they're like sisters to me, they are my best friends and I'm so on my own now!"

I was crying now, "I didn't mean to hurt anybody and I tried to do what everybody wanted and instead I messed it all up and can't get it back."

Sister Bridget offered to talk to the girls but I asked her not to as it might just make things worse than they already are. We agreed to give it to the end of the month and see what way it was then.

Chapter 8

On Friday 29th of January, a number of St Frances''
second year students were taken up by Green River to
gather rushes to make St Bridget's crosses for her feast
day on Feb 1st. Sister Theresa put us in pairs and of
course I was the spare left over, but I explained I didn't
mind as I had been up here many times and lived
nearby.

"Collect as many rushes as possible and bring them
back to the school bus. We will be here for thirty
minutes and then back on the bus to the convent!"

She barked out the orders, and we sat off. The main
group stayed together and picked all the available
rushes in no time, so I ventured off a bit further down
the river bank. I wondered along just thinking about the
spat with Claire and the others and how Madonna and
Niamh were such good mates now. I also thought about
how Beth came for a few days, completely wrecked my
friendships with the other girls and then left without
even saying goodbye, just like the first time she just up
and left me on my own, and I was still waiting for that
phone call too. I had been very stupid and realised that
when you want people to be good friends then you
must treat them with respect. I was having a wee chat
to myself but hadn't gathered any rushes so I decided to
get to the task. I went up to a small clearing and started
to pick the lush green rushes and then saw bigger ones
on the ledge, so I knelt down and reached out to them

without leaning too far over. I started to tug at the rushes when I heard like a crunching sound, before I could do anything the ledge gave way underneath me and I was falling down the steep embankment and into the trees at the bottom. It all happened so quickly. I was tumbling for what seemed like forever, bouncing off stumps and broken branches like a rag doll, when finally I came to an abrupt stop crashing into the base of a big oak tree. I was badly shaken and after a few seconds went to get to my feet. The pain shot through my leg and upper body. I had damaged something and needed help!

"Hello, Help! Can anybody hear me, Help please help!" but there was no response. The pain was getting worse so I called again: "Help! Anybody? Help!" but again there was nothing. I tried to move again but then realised my leg must be broken; It wouldn't move it at all without severe pain. I was also getting sharp pains in the right side of my lower back. I reached my hand round and found I was stuck against a tree stump that was jabbing deeper and deeper into my back. I had to try and ease the pain but my jumper was soaking wet, I couldn't do anything. To my horror it was blood! I was so scared and cried again for help. In what seemed a matter of seconds I was extremely weak, my shouts were very faint as I just wanted to sleep. Just then I heard something and opened my eyes and I could see someone there, it was Sister Bridget but how could it be, she wasn't even on this trip? The lady stayed with me and helped me off the broken stump I had landed on. She made my leg more comfortable and then before she left she gave me a medal or coin shaped thing, she pressed it into my hand and smiled and then she was gone, as I thought to get help.

When I next opened my eyes I was in Southside General Hospital and Mum and Dad were at the bedside;

"Tom she's waking up, quickly go and get somebody, a nurse or doctor!" Mum said as they leaned over me. "Hey Sarah, how are you feeling?" Mum asked, "Don't try to talk pet just take it easy," she continued with her hand on my forehead. A doctor came in and shone a light in my eyes,

"Sarah if you can hear me squeeze my hand" he said. I could hear him but he seemed a million miles away, I could see him, a little blurred but I could see him and Dad in the background.

"Squeeze my hand Sarah if you can hear me," he asked again so I tried and he said, "She's responding, she's moving but we need to take it very slowly."

I kept waking every so often and each time there were different people there. Nana was there one of the times, but when I opened my eyes she went for the door shouting, "Oh Holy Mary she's wakening, she's wakening, Doctor she's wakening, where the hell are you?"

The more times I woke up the better my vision was and I was able to stay awake a little longer, but I couldn't speak, much just short sentences.

Sometime later I came around and was allowed to sit up and sip water. Mum, Dad, Nana and Trina were all there.

"Why is everybody here Mum is something wrong?" I asked.

"You had a bad fall a while ago Sarah and your very lucky to be alive, you lost a lot of blood and had severe head injuries, someone was praying for you pet," she went on, "the family and I have been taking turns sitting at your bedside, hoping and praying that you'd pull through."

I had a look around and some things were a bit strange to me:

"I was getting rushes Mum and I fell, the ledge broke."

Mum interrupted me, "Easy now, just take it easy, you've been through a lot Sarah, Madonna found you and alerted Sister Theresa who got you help. You were unconscious and as luck would have it you landed just a few steps from a jagged tree stump that could have killed you."

I remembered now, "Mum, the Sister helped me, the Sister helped me off the tree stump and moved my leg," Mum smiled,

"She's confused, that was a paramedic Sarah that helped you, the tree stump you hit with your back but luckily you landed clear of it." Mum tried to explain but I knew what happened, I remembered the Sister. What I couldn't explain was why it was so bright and why were there children in the hospital visiting people.

I could see them out in the corridor but it was the middle of the day, why are they not in school?

"Mum why are the children not at school?" I asked.

"Well because its Easter break Sarah, you've been in intensive care for almost 9 weeks, you have been in a semi coma since February and now it's April 10th. The doctors said with the head injuries and loss of blood it's nothing short of a miracle that you're here at all."

I couldn't believe it; "When can I go home?" I asked.

"Well the doctors have a lot more tests to do and there is physiotherapy. You're still very weak and very fragile Sarah. We are hoping there's no permanent damage will come as a result, memory loss things like that," she went on, "Your muscles Sarah are very weak ,your legs will need supports for a time and it will just take time, you're in no rush."

I didn't know what to say or think or do. "We hope to have you home and mobile by the summer holidays by the end of June fingers crossed." Nana spoke;

"I'll lend my stick if I ever find where Sheba buried it," she laughed, "You might get a Granny flat like me, or you'll need your Dad to push you in Britney's buggy?" Trina said,

"It's Whitney Nana." Nana replied;

"Aye whatever, I'm just trying to lighten the mood, God knows that child deserves it!" I said,

"Mum the lady who found me and helped me, does anybody know who she was I'd like to thank her for helping me." Mum butted in again;

"Ok that's enough talking for one session you need to get some sleep, you're raving worse than Aggie and that's saying something, C'mon lie down and get some rest." I tried again:

"But Mum there was a woman, a Sister that..."

Mum again stopped my explanation, "Rest now talk later."

I lay down to rest but I knew there was a lady, and I will prove it somehow.

By the end of April I was well on the way to recovery. I had been out of bed and walked a little though I was shipped up and down to the physio department in a wheelchair. The tests results had been good and I was allowed into the ward proper, and that meant I could have visitors who weren't family. I was a lot better now and able to sit up, read and watch the TV although it was on the other side of the ward.

"Hi ya Bowl head, how are you feeling?"

I knew that voice. I turned to see Claire and Madonna standing there with a magazine and a brown paper bag.

"Yeah Sarah, how's things?" added Madonna.

"I'm alright girls, thank you. It's good to see you, thanks for coming up," I said not knowing what the response would be.

"Look Sarah, we had a stupid argument over silliness and although it seemed important at the time, it really meant nothing when I found you at the bottom of that embankment. I thought you were dead and all I could think of was the argument," Madonna said looking at the floor and the continuing, "I promised Claire and Niamh if you got well again I would sort out our problems because life is too short and things happen so quickly to change things."

Claire joined in, "She's right, we were having a twisting match but all the arguments disappeared when we thought you were badly hurt, we didn't want that, none of us."

I was surprised the girls thought so much of me, but I had to tell them the truth too;

"Over Christmas I was too fond of doing things with Beth and I shouldn't have just thrown away my friendships with you guys, you're my best friends and are here all the time for me. I was wrong and I hope we can be good friends again?"

I waited anxiously for a response, "Of course we can Sarah," said Madonna "What do you think Claire?" she asked.

"Aye I suppose so, if it means me not having to sit beside them other nerds on the bus," Claire giggled.

"Where is Niamh, is she ok to be friends again too do you think?" I asked.

"She's fine just missed out on her science project and she's at home building a Volcano with paper Mache which has to be in by tomorrow so she couldn't come to hospital with us, but she said to tell you to hurry up and get well," Madonna explained. After a little while a nurse came in;

"You have more visitors Sarah, but it's only two or three maximum people per patient so?"

Claire stood up, "We'll head on bowl head and you get well soon, there's a magazine for when you're bored chatting up the doctors!" Madonna added,

"Aye we'll go on here Sarah, oh tell that nurse we're not sisters would you? Thanks see you when you get out." I sat upright;

"Aye, see you soon and thanks again for coming."

The girls disappeared around the corner and out of sight only seconds later to be replaced by Sister Theresa and Sister Bridget.

"Hello Sarah, how you feeling, are you getting better?" asked Sister Theresa.

"I'm improving Sister, I've been in here longer than I thought mind you," I replied.

"You're a very lucky girl Sarah, you had a very bad accident and it could have been a lot worse, you must thank God you're here to tell the tale," said Sister Bridget then she went on, "That was a deep slope and what about that tree stump? Heaven knows what the outcome could have been?"

I was a million miles ahead of them, in my mind I was saying I knew Sister Bridget was there, I knew it.

"Sister Theresa was telling us how lucky you were," Sister Bridget said pulling up a seat, Sister Theresa spoke up;

"The wee girl Madonna heard you shouting and when I got there it didn't look too good but thank god the ambulance men where able to get you to hospital in time, it's probably all a blank to you eh?"

I was confused; "You mentioned the tree stump Sister Bridget?" I asked the Sister.

"Yes Sarah, we went up a few days after the accident and Sister Theresa was showing me where you fell, and we were remarking just how lucky you were," she replied.

"Who was the Sister who came down and helped me? The lady that moved me off the stump and helped me get comfortable?" I asked. The Sisters looked at each other and then back to me,

"There was no Sister there only me Sarah, don't you remember, we were gathering the rushes?" said Sister Theresa. I replied;

"Yes Sister I remember there was a Sister there and she helped me, I thought it was you Sister Bridget, she stayed with me for a little while and helped me away from the tree stump and then left to get help?" Again their faces were drawing blank expressions;

"No Sarah there was no Sister down with you, there was nobody there until the paramedics went down, we couldn't get to you," explained Sister Theresa.

"I was in the convent when the incident took place Sarah, I had the first year Home Economics class so I couldn't have been anywhere near the river at all," said Sister Bridget. Maybe I was imagining it but it was very realistic to me, then again I was out for almost two months,

"Are you alright Sarah?" asked Sister Bridget,

"Eh yeah I'm grand thank you Sister just a little confused. Did you miss me at school? I suppose I'm miles behind in class, it'll take a while to catch up," I said.

"We'll worry about that when you're well enough, as long as you are getting better, that's the main thing," Sister Theresa replied.

"We'll go on and let you get a wee rest and we'll pop in when you get home," said Sister Bridget. "Thanks for coming up and I'll see you when I'm out, cheerio!"

The Sisters left and I sat there trying to replay the events over and over in my head, and although some of the details were very sketchy I still remembered the lady helping me, I couldn't remember her face but I know she was there.

End of May and I was back on my feet and allowed to go home. It had been a long time coming but through the physiotherapy and all the tests, the day had arrived when the Doctors thought I was alright to go. Mum and Trina collected me and in no time I was back in the Grange, I was getting pampered for the first day or two but soon settled back into my own routine. I walked up to Claire's and had Madonna and Niamh over to visit. There was a card from Beth and her Mum but it just said "Get Well Soon," on front and inside 'from Beth.' I asked about going up to St Frances' but Mum said if I waited till Friday she would go up with me and we could visit Nana as well. So I agreed and on Friday morning I was up and good to go when Mum came in from the kitchen.

"Are you ready Sarah? You'll need a jacket it's a bit nippy," she said.

"Aye I'm ready, I've got my fleece and that'll do me alright," I explained. We went up for the bus and got on "2 to Rosnarene," Mum ordered as I went and sat down. After a few seconds Mum joined me and was putting the change in her purse.

"Oh here Sarah, I meant to give you this," she said digging deep into the side of her purse, "This is yours." Mum hand me a gold coin, it was an old coin.

"What's that for?" I asked.

"The Nurse gave me that coin the day we rushed to the hospital, you know, the day of your fall. She gave me your chain and said that you had the coin clasped in your hand?" Mum said, as she got fixed in the seat. I knew it, I wanted to shout out but I also knew that Mum didn't believe me.

"The lady gave that to me," I whispered.

"Lady? What lady?" Mum asked,

"The lady that helped me Mum, I keep telling you about the lady who helped me off the tree stump and stayed with me until I was comfortable. She gave me something into my hand and I remember it was like round, you know like a coin or a medal. This must have been what it was!" I replied examining the coin.

"So what is it and why would she give it to you?" Mum questioned me;

"I don't know why she gave it to me, it looks like old money or something, now do you believe me she was there?" I asked again.

"I can't explain the coin Sarah that's for sure, but nobody on the day saw this woman only you," Mum smirked and raised her shoulders.

"There was a woman Mum, she helped me and gave me this coin, somebody was there and I'll prove it somehow!" I said. I was a little cross that Mum still doubted me but now I had the coin I knew I wasn't imagining things, I knew she was real.

We arrived at the convent and met with Sister Theresa, she was happy to see me and brought me into the class and did all the formalities to my class mates. They gave me a warm welcome and I told them I'd hope to be back before the holidays. Sister Theresa then took me down to the main office as the Mother Superior wanted to see me and Mum. She took us into her office; we had a cup of tea as the Mother got the correct details of my accident from Sister Theresa.

"Hello Sarah, Mrs Corke how are you? Firstly I want to say it's great to see Sarah back up and about again and I believe it's the first time we've met Mrs Corke?" she asked Mum.

"It is indeed Mother, I was here at the open nights and things but you were otherwise engaged on those evenings," Mum explained.

"Yes the open nights and the school functions I play a very small part in, It's nice to meet you and if you ever have any questions or queries please don't hesitate to call or pop in," the Mother replied standing as if to say it was time we went.

"Thank you for the tea Mother," I said and we left for Nanas. Buzz the door bell went and the reply was always the same;

"Hello, who's that?" said Nana.

"It's me and Mum Nana, can we come in or are you playing rummy?" I said jokingly. The buzzer went again letting us into the flat, Nana was by herself, and greeted us saying, "Keep your voice done about the cards, the walls have ears around here, what brings you up today?"

Mum replied, "Sarah was up at the convent saying hello to the Sisters and her friends and we thought we'd call in?" I sat down;

"Well Nana how are you keeping, where's the rest of the crazy gang today?" I said.

"Mary is only away home there and Winnie is away up to get her feet done. Elsa is huffing across the road because I wouldn't go over and look at some curtains or something she bought. I see her gawping around the window blind to see who or what is coming and going from here." Nana turned to me; "You're out and about again anyway Sarah, you must be doing rightly now eh?" she asked.

"Aye flying Nana, sick of sitting about doing nothing though, and by the time I get back to school it'll be time for the summer holidays," I replied.

"I'm sure you'll find something to keep you occupied?" Nana said going into the kitchen "Who's for tea?" she asked while filling the kettle.

"Aye I'll take a drop in my hand just Ma, we got tea up in the Convent but it was that strong you could have stood on it," said Mum as she went into the kitchen to help. I flicked on the telly and made myself comfortable and after a few minutes of channel hopping I went to see what was keeping the tea .As I approached the doorway Mum was telling Nana about the chat we had on the bus about the coin and the woman.

"You shouldn't have gave that child that coin back, if you had kept it or dumped it then you'd have saved yourself a lot of hassle, Sarah doesn't remember half of what happened and it'll only make her start thinking about it," Nana said.

"I don't know Ma, what do you think the crack is with this woman, Sarah is convinced there was somebody there?" Mum replied.

"All in her head I'm telling you, she got a right bad toss and hit her head, the child must be dreaming or just dazed, sure they gave her that old face mask thing that day too, so she was out of her head!" Nana retorted.

"Aye I know that but she's still at it the day coming up here on the bus, and how do you explain the coin, it's not even a proper coin it's as old as Methuselah?" Mum asked but Nana just shrugged;

"God knows were she got it from, Sale of the Century is on."

I quickly sat down as Nana came in and changed the channel, "No offence ladies but I'm watching my programmes so if you want to make tracks for the bus I'll see you on Sunday?"

Mum and I took the hint and went home.

I had an early night but while in bed I figured I'm going to do a bit of detective work of my own, like my heroes from a couple of years ago. I know nobody believes me about the woman so I'm going have to find her myself and prove it, just like they would on

131

Charlie's Angels. Saturday morning I went up to Claire's and told her my plan. She wasn't convinced it was a great idea and said she didn't see the point of looking for somebody who might not even be real, but she was willing to lend a hand where required. We rang Madonna and Niamh and recruited them as well. The girls arrived in the afternoon and we decided we would put our heads together and see what we have.

"A coin, a woman, and an accident that happened roughly three months before. Where should we start?" I asked, and the decision was Green River so off we went. It was only a short walk from Claire's and we were there in no time, we walked along the river bank and towards where I fell but there was nothing or nobody to see. We went up onto the embankment and looked down into the trees and bushes at the bottom but there was nothing. Claire said;

"What exactly are we looking for?" Madonna and Niamh both looked at me.

"I'm not really sure, just something that might give us a clue to the woman?" I said raising my shoulders then continuing, "How can we get down into the trees?"

Claire laughed, "Face first like you did is the quickest way," I just stared at her.

"Sorry just a joke, I don't know I've never been down in the trees at the bottom," Claire said.

"I've only been here once," said Madonna, and Niamh said,

"There must be some way down; didn't the paramedics get down to you?"

I nodded, "Yeah that's right there has to be a way down."

As we looked around for a path or tack down, along came Mickey Thompson;

"How's it going there girls, are you out on a date, the four of you like?" he said as he stood arms folded. "Nah were looking for something and it's none of your business so buzz off," I said.

"Well look who it is, the high diving champion from the Green River Olympics!" he said, smirking. "Watch your mouth or you'll need a hospital bed!" Claire said.

"Take some bed to hold you," he replied. "Are you better then, because the fall didn't help your looks any," he went on.

"Go and get a life Mickey, your a pain in the ass," said Madonna. Then Niamh chimed in;

"Do you be around here much Mickey?" he laughed.

"Duh I live here don't I?" Niamh replied, "Aye but I mean down here at the river, have you ever been down in the trees at the bottom there?"

Mickey looked confused, "Our Colin went down there once to get logs to make them Christmas things, you know you stick tinsel on them and drill a hole for a candle, what are they called?" he asked.

"Eh try a log, a Christmas log?" said Claire with a big grin.

"Thank you for that lardy, anyway he went down to get logs but there wasn't any apart from the tree stumps and they weren't worth doddle," Mickey said, putting his hands in his pockets before continuing, "What do want to get down there for? I could find out off Colin and let you know, only if you tell me what you're doing, deal?" he asked.

"Deal," said Niamh with her fingers crossed behind her back and smiling over at Claire, Madonna and me. "Right I'll find out and meet you up here tomorrow, then you tell me what you're looking for?" Mickey said.

"Aye tomorrow evening after mass and that and then all will be revealed," replied Claire.

"I'm away here I'll see you dolls tomorrow, don't miss me too much!" Mickey was blowing kisses at Claire and laughing while she pretended to make herself sick by putting her fingers down her throat. After he went out of sight we decided that nobody could know what we were trying to find and so we agreed to keep it purely between the four of us.

Next evening after mass and Sunday lunch I made my way up to the park and met up with Claire. Niamh arrived but Madonna couldn't make it as she had chores and other things that she couldn't get out of. We waited for a while and true to his word Mickey appeared

"How's the girls today, sorry to keep you waiting but I'm worth waiting for eh?" was his introduction.

"Did you find out the way down to the trees?" Claire asked sharply.

"All in good time, first I want to know what's down there that you lot are looking for, I think that was the deal right?" he said smugly.

"The deal was you tell us the way, and then we will take you with us and show you what we were looking for," said Niamh.

"Oh I'm going too am I, that's great news, though what would people say around the town, Mickey Thompson went into the trees last Sunday with three girls, I might never come out alive. What if the big one fell on me?" he sniggered.

"He hasn't a clue, he's just pulling your leg Billy, he knows nothing about the trees or how to get down there, he's a mouth piece," Claire snapped again.

"I do know the way and it's very simple, if you follow the wee path on around by the clearing there are old railway sleepers and they're bedded into the ground, they act like steps or stairs right down to the bottom, which is handier than the way you rolled down," Mickey continued, "So what are you lot going down there for?"

Niamh said, "Well now that you've told us your part of the deal then we'll come clean," she looked at me and Claire: "We're looking for Woodrow, a New Zealand woodpecker, it's worth thousands of pounds and it was seen in the area last week."

Mickey frowned, "There's no woodpecker in the Grange are you lot mad or what, where did hear such nonsense, did you tell them this when you cracked you nut open down there?" he said turning to me.

"Nobody knows about it. We will catch it and get the reward, the problem is that it's wild and will tear the skin of anyone that goes near it," Niamh said.

"And you're taking Claire along because there's enough there for him to chew on for a month?" Mickey laughed. "Somebody is making fools out of you and if you think I'm going with you on a wild goose chase then forget it." Niamh was in again:

"There's no goose just a woodpecker!"

Mickey replied, "There's no wood pecker either, you're a pile of weirdo's." He clambered onto his bike, "I never heard anything like it, Woodpecker from New Zealand you say, must have cost it a fortune in the taxi to get here; sure they can't fly?"

We both looked at Niamh, "Duh that's why it's rare, it can fly, there's only one of them in the world." she said. Mickey said:

"Did you hear about the rare breed of girl going about, called the absolute gipe, I can see three of them now, don't move till I get my camera!" he said as he started pedalling away. I couldn't believe Niamh had come up with such a story;

"It's in the News of the World about the woodpecker but it escaped from London Zoo so I just changed the story a wee bit. I didn't think he'd go for it but he did so let's go," she said climbing off the roundabout and going towards Green river. We followed in hot pursuit up the path and past the clearing to where I fell, but just as we headed for the sleepers and the steps down, the creaking sound of bicycle brakes broke the silence. I looked up and there was Mickey;

"There's no woodpecker is there?" he said then turning the bike away, "just like there are no steps." We

136

looked and there was nothing only a big grassy knoll and a large drop down to the trees.

"So where are the steps? You wee slime ball?"Claire yelled.

"I knew you would try and set me up so I told you a load of rubbish, just like you told me. A flying Woodpecker do you think I'm stupid?"

Niamh butted in, "Ok, ok you're right there's no bird, so if you know the way then show us and we'll tell you the truth." Mickey gave a wry smile, "Now that's more like it, c'mon and keep up," he moved off and we followed. After a few minutes he said, "There that's the way down." He pointed at what looked like an opening in the hill side; "Years ago people would go for nice wee walks around here and down through the caves, you mightn't fit mind you," he said nodding at Claire. "They will take you out near the bottom, that's really where the sleeper steps are, go and look."

I went over and this time I could see pretty rugged wooden steps leading down a steep curve. "He's right, there are steps," I shouted back.

"C'mon then," Niamh said as she linked onto Mickey arm.

"What are you at?" he growled.

"Och c'mon you know rightly I fancied you from the New Years Eve party and how else were we going to get together and get some privacy?" Niamh smiled at Mickey then went on, "You're not shy are you?" she pulled his arm, "C'mon into the cave and the girls will keep an eye out in case anybody comes."

137

Mickey's face went as white as a sheet, "Get off will you! I'm not eh, I don't like the, I've got to get back, I've stuff to do for my Dad," he said turning the bike around in a flash and getting away as quick as possible.

"Just a wee kiss then Mickey," Niamh shouted, but Mickey wasn't stopping - he was out of sight in no time, leaving Claire, me and Niamh in fits of laughter.

Chapter 9

After the laughter had died down, we went into the mouth of the cave and could see the steep steps spiralling out of sight, "Are we going down?" asked Claire.

"I'm up for it if you are?" said Niamh. I got to admit I was a little scared but couldn't show it.

"Might as well see what's down there," I said starting into the cave. As we went down it got darker but not dark enough that we couldn't see, and soon we reached the bottom, the brightness came back as we stood looking onto the forest floor. There were a lot of broken tree stumps and branches on the ground but no sign of any life. "We'll have to go in a bit deeper girls and see what we can find," I said confidently, though inside a little wary.

"Well we now know the way down so we could come back when Madonna's here eh? She wouldn't want to miss it," suggested Niamh.

"You're scared aren't you? You are, you're bricking it!" laughed Claire. "It's only the woods like, c'mon and see what there is to see, I don't fancy them steps a second day," she said as she walked off with Niamh and me close behind. We walked and walked and there were more trees and more trees but after a while a space, not much just a clear patch.

"I think we should split up this is going to take all day," was Claire's next suggestion, but we agreed to stick as one unit much to her disappointment. After another few yards we decided to go back and try another day as it was getting late, needless to say we moved a lot quicker on the way back and soon got to the cave. "Look!" shouted Niamh, "look there on the ground!" We ran over to her and she was pointing, "There on the ground, the coins!" she said. There on the ground at the mouth of the cave were two coins, exactly the same as the other one I had, "How did they get there, they weren't there when we came down," Niamh said bending to pick them up.

"Leave them there Niamh, they're not ours and I bet someone has put them there as some sort of trap, it's too much of a coincidence that those coins should be there and match the one that Sarah has, there's something not right here," said Claire, her large round rosy face not so rosy anymore. "It must mean something, I'm getting out of here," she said.

"It means I've got a gold coin that might be worth something, that's what it means," said Niamh lifting the coins. I added; "It also means whoever put those coins there knows we are here and could be watching us right at this very minute?"

Claire bolted through the entrance of the cave her big frame shaking the ground:

"I'm going, I'll see you at the top if whatever's down there doesn't get you first!" She was out of sight and pounding up the sleepers when Niamh shouted, "What if the woman is in the cave waiting on us going up?" The pounding got louder as Claire appeared round the corner of the cave again even whiter than before;

"Never thought of that. I'll wait with you guys, save you going up on your own like," she said panting for breath. We figured we'd go back up now and keep a coin each and also to keep everything secret until next Saturday when we'd come back with Madonna and a little more time to explore.

On Monday we told Madonna all about the coins and the cave and how we were going down again on Saturday, though Claire wasn't so keen but she said she was up for it just to prove she wasn't afraid.

I went back up to the Convent on Wednesday and chatted to Sister Bridget. I was doing my detective work because Claire was convinced whatever or whoever we were looking for might be some sort of spirit and that was beginning to sway my mind as well.

"Hello Sarah, it's great to see you again, are you feeling better now?" said the Nun.

"Aye, I'm grand now Sister thank you, are you free for a wee bit I was hoping to ask you something?" I replied.

"Surely Sarah come in." She showed me into her room and we sat down. "What's bothering you then?" she asked.

"Well Sister ever since I had my fall, I've wanted to try and find the woman who helped me, now I know nobody believes me but the lady gave me a coin that day and I had it in my hand at the hospital." I took the coin out of my pocket, "Here it is look it's real and so is the lady but everybody thinks I'm crazy. My friend thinks it might be a spirit or something from like years ago and I was wondering do you know anybody that maybe had an accident there or.."

Sister Bridget stopped me; "Slow down Sarah, firstly the fact that your friend thinks there might be a ghost or spirit is fascinating though without some concrete evidence it's very unlikely. As for stories of people having accidents and things like that, the Convent has stood in Rosnarene for hundreds of years so there is bound to be a tall tale or two, how truthful they are is a different story?" she smiled, "Your Nana or somebody of that age would be better at telling the stories of Rosnarene."

I nodded, "Aye but sure Nana tells me lots of things but most of it is just in her mind, she doesn't know if she's coming or going most the time." We both laughed;

"Well Sarah I'm going to have to get back to class now and I'm sorry I don't have a wonderful story to tell you, but good luck in finding your Guardian Angel."

Sister Bridget stood up, "Why did you call her that Sister, My Guardian Angel?" I asked.

"It's just a figure of speech child dear, I think everybody has somebody watching out for them and maybe this lady is yours?" she patted me on the head, "because you can't see something doesn't mean it's not there. I got to run, pop in again Sarah, cheerio!"

I was leaving now too, "Thanks for the chat Sister; I'll call at Nana's while I'm up here and see if she can help me, see you later!" I went out and down the short walk to the sheltered housing and Nana was out in the front garden;

"Hi Nana, what are up to today?" I said "Hello Sarah, how are you, you didn't see Sheba on your way down?" she said.

"Nah Nana, have you lost her again?" I asked jokingly.

"That dog is useless, there's something not right with her, I put her out a dish of stuff yesterday and she hasn't touched it, somebody else must be feeding her. Are you coming in for a while? It won't be long mind you because I'm going to get my eyes tested," she walked off into the flat.

"How could I refuse such an invite?" I whispered following her in and asking, "Nana you've been around these parts a long time, was there ever anything strange or weird that happened, anybody have an accident or be murdered in the forest?" Nana turned quickly;

"Did you say somebody got murdered in the forest, when, who was it?"

Nana went for the rosary beads, "What has this place come to, you're not safe anywhere these days. I'll get myself a gun and keep it under the bed, that's the next thing..."

I intervened; "Calm down Nana I meant years ago, was there anything strange happened years ago? Not now!"

She sighed: "Sarah you'll be the death of me, what are trying to do telling me somebody was murdered in the forest and then saying you were only codding, sure I might as well have keeled over and then where would you have been?" she tutted and went on, "You'd have

143

been ringing Kennedys and ordering my a wooden overcoat!"

I had a little giggle, "Nana you didn't listen to me I asked was there anything like that happened years ago, see years ago?" she was a bit more relaxed now.

"Strange things happen around this place all the time, just yesterday I was in Mary's next door and one of her clan had brought this paper stuff they had got in America. You pull these two bits of paper apart and you put the sticky bit on you leg or ocster and after a couple of seconds you whip it away and it takes the hair off your legs. Well now I ask you did you ever hear the like of it? This young lassie was telling me and Mary all about it and yesterday evening I was sitting here watching Blockbusters when I heard this scream from next door." Nana got up to demonstrate and then went on, "I was out through the door and into Marys thinking in under God what has happened and she opened the door, she was as white as a sheet. I followed her in and said tell me here Mary what the heavens has happened you?" Nana was very serious and I was worried.

"What had happened Nana?" I asked.

"Here dear, hadn't Mary decided to try out the paper stuff on her; she was trying to take the hair off her chin with it. Two hours and twenty eight minutes we were in the casualty and Mary had all sorts of creams rubbed into the red marks on her chin and neck, but she's rightly today because I was in earlier and she had the bandages off, and to tell the truth there's not a hair on her chin now so they must work?"

144

I was in stitches in the corner but did my best to hide it.

"What do you want to know these things for anyway Sarah?" Nana asked.

"I'm doing this like History project for when I go back to school so I'm trying to get some local stories, do you know any others Nana?" I replied.

"The one that sticks out in my mind is the time the Gypsy woman called at our house, och it must be thirty years ago now. I went to the door and she had this suitcase selling all sorts of clothes, pegs and liquids for ailments and things. Your Granda always had sore backs and the Gypsy told me she had this stuff that had worked all kinds of miracles, you just rub it in at night and you'd be grand in a day or two." Nana laughed and said, "Anyhow I bought this potion off her and that night I said to Willie try a drop of that stuff on your back and see if it eases it any," Nana went on, "away he went into the bathroom and returned to go to bed but the smell of him was tara, I said till him You must need a good read out but he told me it was the potion I'd gave him. So the next morning he was up and the whole bottom of his back was going mad with itch, so down we went to the surgery and got him checked." Nana was off on one now smiling and giggling away to herself, "It turned out your Gypsy woman was using the horses wee from up at the camp and putting it into bottles as a mystery potion! Your Granda used to tell that story for years and always would say it's a good job he hadn't the toothache or a bad throat!" Nana let a big laugh out of her, "Agh them was the days. That's

145

before your Mum came along, though I don't know if you could tell that in your project?"

I was nearly sick and I don't think Nana was going to tell me anything remotely close to what I wanted to know.

"What time is the appointment at the Opticians at Nana?" I asked.

"Oh sugar I forgot about that, it's time I was away. You may see yourself out there love and I'll get myself ready. Sure call in again when you have more time?" she disappeared into the back bedroom and I headed off for the Grange, my book of information empty but an insight into life in Rosnarene very much fulfilled.

After school I went up to Claire's and she had done better than me, she had taken the coin to her Mums brother who said it was an old foreign coin of some sort but wasn't sure what it was, he knew it was old and guessed it might be French. Claire said he collected old things like coins and medals and was usually quite good with his guessing. This made the mystery even worse, now we had a mystery woman in a forest in the Irish countryside who was throwing around coins that were years old and from France. We all got together and nobody had a clue or even a suggestion as to how we could connect the information. Saturday morning and early as possible Madonna and Niamh arrived in the Grange. We called at Claire's and were walking down towards the Green River when Mickey and Colin Thompson came out of the park. It was the first time ever Mickey was quiet:

"Hi girls," said Colin.

"Hello lads, how are you keeping?" asked Claire.

"Aye grand thanks, are you heading for a walk by the river? Do you mind if we tag along?"

He asked, "No, not at all," said Niamh and she winked at Mickey.

"I'm going home, I've stuff to do," said Mickey quick as a flash.

"Can't it wait till after Mickey, sure it's the weekend?" Claire said knowing Mickey was uncomfortable. "Nah it can't wait and nobody asked for your input, is that a new chain? It looks just like the one on our bog," he said. Claire quickly covered up her neck with her jacket;

"It's just a necklace; I see you haven't learned any manners yet!"

Colin butted in, "You should be well used to him by now, Mickey shut up for a change eh?"Claire smiled. "What are grinning at, do you think there's a chance you might go swapping slabbers with our boy down the caves? I suppose he could do with getting his face washed," Mickey said as he moved a safe distance back. "Are you coming or not?" asked Niamh moving closer to Mickey.

"Nah I'm not going anywhere with you freaks, c'mon Colin or I'll tell Da!" Colin pushed Mickey; "You're such a child; I'll maybe catch up with you later girls when he's not about?"

The Thompson boys left and we went on up the path leaving the Green River behind and towards the embankment, then a little further to the entrance of the cave.

There was no hesitation this time, we just plodded on down the wooden steps and out at the bottom.

"Which way are we going today?" asked Niamh, while Claire scoured the ground.

"What are you looking for?" asked Madonna.

"Coins, the last day we came down there was nothing here, and when we came back there were two coins. I'm just making sure there is nothing here to start with." said Claire.

"We'll split into groups of two and go in both directions, that way we'll cover the area twice as quickly," was my suggestion and the others agreed. I would go with Niamh, and Claire with Madonna. So we set off through the trees and soon the other pair was out of sight. We walked for ages but saw nothing just a few old broken trees and stumps so we made our way back. When we arrived at the cave again Claire was there but no Madonna. "Where's Madonna?" we both asked Claire, and she explained; "We walked for a long way just chatting and suddenly bounding through the trees we could see something. We waited and then realised it was a large dog. Madonna shouted to me to run so I did, and when I got into the clearing I looked back and she wasn't there, neither was the dog." She sniffed, "I told you not to come back down here, there is something not right and now Madonna is missing. What are we going to do?"

Claire was shaking and I wasn't feeling too brave either but Niamh said; "We have to go and look for her, she couldn't have disappeared like!"

Claire piped up, "I'm not going into those trees again!"

Niamh got angry, "So what Claire? We just dump on our friend and leave her here, some mate you are?" Claire thought and said; "I'm just a bit nervous that's why I got this," she opened her jacket and revealed this big wooden cross on a thick chain. "I saw it on the telly one time that if you wear one of these you'll be safe."

I found it funny and explained, "It's not Dracula we're trying to find..." but as I was speaking Madonna called out through the trees and we ran to her. She was hobbling and her jeans were torn at the bottom revealing a cut ankle.

"What happened you Madonna? Where did you go?" Claire asked.

"When the dog came and we started to run I saw it was gaining on me, so I cut off to the side behind a big oak tree and when the dog ran past I went to make my get away but my foot was wedged between broken branches on the ground. The branches were too heavy and my heel was stuck fast." Madonna showed us her heal and was bleeding a little, and then she went on, "I couldn't shout out to Claire as the dog was still around so I was trapped." We waited in anticipation, Madonna turned to me:

"Sarah the woman you saw is very real, she is old, her clothes are black and dirty and she is very frightened. She freed my foot and when I asked her who she was, she ran off and she is the one with the coins, she threw the coin on the ground beside me and then clapped her hands together and the dog ran to her and they went into the woods."

I was happy then scared, then happy. Somebody else had seen the woman and she really did exist. Our focus had changed now from trying to find a person till trying to find out who or what the person is. "Didn't she say anything at all?" I asked but Madonna said, "No, she just looked strangely at me and was gone in seconds."

Madonna opened her hand and there was another of the gold coins. "Do you now where we can find her if we went to her now?" asked Niamh. "No," said Madonna, but Claire had a flash of intelligence; "It's simple, one of us go into the woods and pretend we are injured or hurt and she will come to help us, when she does we grab her!"

Madonna snapped, "We can't do that, run around grabbing people for no reason, she is frightened enough without us lot trying to kidnap her. The first part of your plan is good, but if she has seen us she'll know we're up to something. We need somebody new."

We thought for a while but nobody else knows what we're doing so who would be trustworthy enough to go along with the plan. "How about your brother Luke?" Madonna said looking at Niamh. "Nah he's too gobby, the whole town would know about it, what about that boy we met earlier, his brother said he was down here before?"

Niamh was brighter than we gave her credit for, she couldn't make a Shepherds' pie but she was a sharp thinker. We went back up to the park and Colin was there with Mickey and we had a chat with him while Niamh kept Mickey busy chasing him around the roundabout shouting, "Catch and kiss that's the game Mickey, catch and kiss," with Mickey running round and round screaming,

"Get away from me you sicko!" We told Colin we were doing a mock first aid test for the convent and needed a person to pretend to be trapped and injured in the trees and then we would find them and rescue them, but Colin said; "No way, not down in the trees. I'll be your patient up on the grass but not down in the trees."

Claire asked, "Why not down in the trees, what's wrong with down in the trees?" but Colin just shrugged, "I'm not going down in the trees, I was down there before Christmas and I'm not going down again."

We tried to persuade him but the verdict was always the same? After another hour or so the Thompsons were gone and we just sat trying to think of someone, when Baz appeared.

"Hi Billy, Claire, Niamh, Madonna," he said giving us all a name check.

"How's it going Baz?" was the collective reply.

"Any crack with you lot today, I was bored to tears over at home so my Ma is down in your house Billy and I came over with her," he said.

"Do you fancy giving us a hand with our school project Baz, we need somebody who can act and Billy told us your quite good at most stuff?" Claire said all gooey eyed.

"Aye I'll give it a go if you want. What do I have to do?"

We told him the same story as we told Colin and he agreed to do it. We went back down the wooden steps and into the woods with Madonna leading the way to where she had encountered the lady. "Right anywhere around here, you go and pretend to be hurt and we'll find you," Madonna told Baz, and off he went. "I'll shout when I'm ready ok?" he said as he ran deeper into the woods. A few minutes later we heard; "Help, help I'm trapped!"

It was Baz obviously, so we watched him rolling around on the ground from a few metres away waiting for the lady, but there was nothing. We were just about to move when Claire screamed and belted past us towards Baz.

"That's very realistic Claire, give him the kiss of life when you get there," I said, but Claire turned and pointed making us turn too and there she was behind us, long hair, black jumper, an old tatty skirt with a pinafore over it, on her feet she had what looked like knee boots. She had a scraggy old face with dirt deep into the wrinkled expression.

There was a silence as we stood looking at each other and suddenly she turned and started into the woods; "C'mon!" shouted Niamh and we started after her. She was quick over the ground for an old lady but we kept her in sight and she went round a thicket and into a tin shack buried among the trees. We stopped and waited, Claire and Baz still back in the woods.

"Maybe we should go now?" suggested Niamh, but Madonna and I wanted to speak to the old lady, so we went to what was supposed to be the doorway. Inside was a small fire smouldering and we could see the old lady cowering in the corner.

"Hello, are you ok?" I asked but she didn't answer.

"We just wanted to talk to you," said Niamh, but again she just stared. After a little while she moved to the doorway and pushed out a leather purse, in it was eight more coins.

"What's your name? I'm Sarah," I said. "This is Niamh and Madonna, you helped me a long time ago, I fell and you saved me do you remember?"

She looked at me and nodded her head. At least now I know she understood me.

"Can you talk?" I asked, and again she nodded.

"My name is Ellen," she said in a whisper. "You must leave here now and never come back, you must never tell anyone I'm here," she said.

"Who are you? Where do you live? You helped me and I want to thank you, is there anything I or we can get you or do for you?" I asked, but the old lady seemed very frightened, more frightened of us than we were of her. "Do you want some of this?"Madonna said, opening her lunchbox and setting out her sandwiches. In a flash Ellen came to the door and snatched the food and devoured it in seconds.

"You're hungry eh?" said Madonna. We looked round; it was obvious that Ellen had been living here, as there were some old clothes in the corner and old food packages strewn around. The fire was almost out but the ground was completely bare of any kind of grass which meant she had been here a long time. I went to enter the hovel to give her more sandwiches when the dog blocked he doorway, its teeth stripped ready to pounce;

"Sheba! Down Sheba!" snarled Ellen, and the dog immediately retreated. We gave her more food and she came to the entrance and started to ask us questions.

"What do you want? Who are you and how did you find me?"

I explained that after my fall the girls and I had set ourselves the task of finding her and proving to everybody that she was here. "You saved my life and I want to thank you, you also helped Madonna when she got trapped but nobody believes you are here." I continued, "When I tell them you are here then they will believe me, everybody will believe me."

Ellen grabbed my arm, "No, you must not tell anybody, not ever. I am not allowed to be here, they don't like me being here so you must never say!"

Ellen was very scared. It was getting late and so we asked if we didn't say anything to anyone about her being here could we come again and visit her, maybe bring her clothes or food. Ellen was still very wary of us and although I don't think she trusted us, she agreed and we left her alone in her space and went back up through the cave to the Grange. In the park we met Claire and Baz who weren't very happy and asked us about the old lady but we told them we lost her, and when Baz left to go home we told Claire the truth and that we were ok to go to see Ellen again as long as nobody else ever knew she was there. We had now developed a whole new investigation. Who really was Ellen, why was she down in the woods living in that hovel and more importantly who are the people who don't like her being here?

On Sunday we had lunch at our house and Mum said, "I thought when Trina and Whitney come over we could collect your Nana and go for a nice walk, it's a nice day. What do you say Sarah?" I had to think quickly;

"I'm already going up to the park today Mum, I have planned to meet up with the girls and go for a walk," I said, but Mum was quick to ask;

"Where are you going, you've been meeting up with the girls and walking a lot lately. I hope your not up at that embankment, you know you're not allowed up there, one accident is plenty." She said, eyebrows raised. "We just get bored sitting about and we never plan our wee walks we just go wherever we decide at the time," I replied.

"Well don't make any plans for next Sunday," Mum said, and I nodded in agreement. I dried the dishes, put some food into my back pack and called for Claire, she said her Mum was quizzing her as well. We met the others and went back down to see Ellen making sure nobody was following us. When we got near the shack, the dog was outside and started barking as we came closer but Ellen appeared in the doorway and he stopped instantly.

"Hi Ellen, how are you today?" I asked.

"Who are you, you there the big one, who are you?" Ellen said pointing a crooked finger at Claire. "It's alright Ellen she is our friend she is with us, we brought you some food?" I said holding out an apple I took from the house and some bread rolls. Ellen was slow to take the food but soon started eating the dry bread and disappearing inside the shack with the apple.

"Could we come in?" asked Niamh and to my surprise Ellen said, "Yes, come inside but don't touch anything, I know what's in here."

Claire looked at me, "We don't but," as she clutched the big cross in her hand. It was pretty dark inside apart from beams of sunlight through the spaces in the trees; there were old blankets on the floor, some old newspapers and a couple of old saucepans, one without a handle. There was food boxes stacked in one corner, things like oatmeal and porridge. It didn't smell great in the hovel either and there were some old clothes in the other corner and a small suitcase. When we got inside we just looked at each other and Ellen said;

"This is all I've got left now, this place and the coins, nothing else."

We were still looking at the state of the place. "How long have you been here and how do you survive, what are the coins for?"

I had loads of questions for Ellen. "I've been here for thirty years and I look after myself, I have to. They won't let me up there, I'm not allowed up there and if they knew I was here I would get put away again. I won't let them so I just stay here." She stumbled around, "What do you want with me now?" she asked staring at us.

"We could maybe help you, you helped us? You don't have to live here; you could get a flat in the sheltered housing. There are flats at the Convent you know," suggested Madonna.

"No, I just told you they don't want me up there!" Ellen snapped and I asked,

"Who, who doesn't want you up there?"

Ellen turned to me, "The Nuns, they don't want me here; they say I must go but I didn't want to go, but they make me!"

I was totally intrigued by Ellen. Niamh had brought a flask of soup for her and we started to chat; "Tell us about yourself Ellen and how you came to be down here."

Ellen sat down on the blankets, "I was an orphan child left at the Convent by my Mother. I suppose I must have been four or five and that was in 1932.They let me stay with them and I grew up in the convent doing chores, I would do the floors and dishes, help prepare the meals and clean the Mother's quarters and office," she looked up at us, "it wasn't much but I got to know some people outside the convent and would go into town sometimes, but I was always on my own as I hadn't got family here. I never had any money or anything of my own as the Sisters and the Mother looked after me, I never wanted for anything either." she pulled the blankets over her legs. "But that was a long time ago."

We were all sat around her on the ground. "What happened then Ellen that changed things?" asked Madonna.

Ellen sighed, "I was nearly 21 and one night on my way back to the convent with some shopping a lady approached me and asked me to get her something from the Convent, she said she would give me money for it. I never had my own money and so I did it."

Ellen looked a little frightened. "When the Mother heard what I did she threw me out of the Convent and I went into town, but the word soon spread I was a thief and what was worse I had stolen from the Sisters of Saint Frances at the Convent, the ones whom had taken me in and brought me up. I was a disgrace to the community and it was suggested I leave town or be run out of town. So I went to the woman and asked her to come and help me explain, but she pretended she never even knew me. So I had the choice of leave or hide, and that's why I'm here and can't go back up there. As far as the Sisters are concerned I went and thirty years on they're no wiser."

Ellen smiled, "I've been up and looked at them once or twice and they never even knew. When you fell, you attracted too much attention to the wood. I helped you and went away as the Sisters were about. The only other time anybody came down here was a lad lifting firewood and he must have broke the world record when he sat eyes on me, to be honest I needed the wood more than him," she smiled, and revealed some pretty bad teeth. "I sort of hoped someday somebody might actually find me and so when you passed out I gave you one of the coins, and I guess as you're here, it worked!"

Claire spoke up, "The other coins, at the cave?"

Ellen said, "I watched you go into the woods and then left them there; you can run for a chubby girl I'll give you that. My old dog has less good teeth than I have but he looks scary, how's your ankle?" she said turning to Madonna.

"It's ok thank you, still cut but its fine."

Ellen said; "That's the life story, so it's time you girls went back to where you belong, thank you for the food. Pop in if you're passing and remember if anybody asks you've never saw me."

We got to our feet and went, but I had a feeling we would be visiting again soon. I owed Ellen a lot and I felt she wanted us to find her. I had to repay her, and trying to clear her name might just be the way.

Chapter 10

Mum and I decided I was ok to go back to school on the Monday, and I met Claire at the bus stop as usual and we headed for St Frances'. On the way we chatted about Ellen and the whole day before. In the classroom Madonna and Niamh were also talking about her. At lunch time we gathered down at the football pitches, "What's the plan then?" asked Niamh. "We can't just go down in the woods every week and bring food for an old lady and pretend she doesn't exist the rest of the week?" she said. Madonna joined in, "She isn't old."

Claire and I looked shocked "What? How is she not old? You saw her yesterday Madonna?" I said. "Yeah I saw her but she said she was four or five in 1932, and if my mathematics is any good she is only about fifty nine now, that's not that old. Maybe living in the trees with lack of food, clean water and the weather hasn't helped but she isn't old," Madonna replied, and she was right fifty nine isn't old.

"My Nana is in her seventies and my Mum is almost forty six," I told the girls. Then suddenly Claire spoke up, "If she is only fifty nine that would mean the Mother Superior who is in charge of the Convent now would have been here when Ellen was working here? How old do you think the Mother is?" she asked.

"I'd say eighty" said Madonna.

"Nah about seventy eight," I guessed.

160

"Eighty four," said Niamh.

"Well if any of you are right it would mean that the Mother was..."

Claire started to count fingers and mumble, "she would have been in her mid to late twenties when Ellen came." said Madonna.

"Aye that's what I was going to say," said Claire ramming her hands in her pocket.

"I think somebody should ask her, but how can we without raising any suspicion?" I said.

"We'll have to think of something ladies or someone who can help us," said Madonna with a wry smile as the bell rang to signify the end of the lunch break. "See what you can find out and we'll chat again tomorrow or Wednesday," said Claire as she went off to her own year group and classes.

The next few days were quiet, with each of us unable to come up with anything or anybody that could help. On the Thursday I went to visit Nana, and the other old ladies were in the flat when I got there;

"Hi ladies, are you alright, any word of any of you getting married and giving us a day out?"I said jokingly.

"I don't think anybody would take us, unless they fancy old smoothy over there," said Winnie nodding at Mary.

"Do you know that time I was in the Hospital after waxing my face they must have done something to my ears because I can hear the grass growing now," laughed Mary. Elsa and Nana were in the kitchen so I decided to test the water a little with the other two.

"Have you lived in Rosnarene a long time Mary, or what about you Winnie?" I asked.

"Only all my life child, my Father and Mother always lived here and I never had any reason to go anywhere else, though Winnie only came up here after the war sometime, I mind her coming to the town and thinking she was lady muck, but she soon lost that chip off her shoulder. There are no heirs or graces in this wee town. Everybody knew everybody else's business and helped out where they could," said Mary.

Winnie smiled, "Aye that's right I moved here in the forties and Jasus they were tough times. I mind I had fox fur hat and I thought I was no miss." She laughed loudly, "One Sunday me and the man were out for a walk and it was the summertime, a nice evening and we sat down by the meadow up at the Mill. I had the hat on because his nibs told me it made me look like one of them film stars. Anyway we were sitting on the grass and looking into each others eyes while the rest of the world went by, so I took my hat off and let my hair down. Up from the Mill come old Patsy McGrath, he had been out with the whippet hunting Rabbits and before any of us could say anything didn't the old dog see my Fox hat sticking up out of the grass. Well in a flash he snapped the hat and started tearing fadges out of it while I sat there balling and crying and old Patsy tried to get it off him."

She wiped her eyes with her sleeve; "You can look back at things and laugh but it was no laughing matter at the time!" Then she sighed, "Old Patsy and my old fella Frank are both dead and away." Mary chimed in,

"What you never have you never miss, I had my share of romances but never put the ring on me."

I enjoyed listening to the stories but was still hoping they would shed some light on Ellen.

Nana and Elsa came in and joined the conversation, "Are you chatting about men again Mary, you'll go blind as well as deaf," laughed Nana While Elsa got herself settled on the sofa.

"Did any of you young ladies ever work in your long lives or were you always looked after by the men?" I asked.

"How dare you, you wee pup, I worked in the linen Mill from I was fourteen years of age till I met your Granda," said Nana.

"Aye she did, I was in it for a wee while myself and mind her working away like a good 'un. I moved on after a while to the factory and ended up in Walsh's Drapery shop, which would have been ol' Paddy Walsh at that time now the son is running it," said Mary. Winnie worked as a shop girl too in her early days but that was before moving to Rosnarene. Then Elsa started talking:

"I worked in the cheese factory out in Finagate and my Father used to take some good hearty laughs at me coming in with the White wellies on me. I had a wee net cap, it was all about keeping clean in case anything fell off you into the big vats," she said.

"Did you have net under your chin?" giggled Winnie.

"There were no bins inside the factory," said Elsa looking a little confused.

"She's taking over from Mary in the deaf club," said Nana as Elsa went on;

"I left there because I couldn't stick the smell of the place, it smelled like deep blitter in the warm months but then I ended up working about eight or ten mile away up at Lough side where the boats come in. Do you know this it smelled blooming worse up there!" she laughed.

"You think some of you lot could of got a job up here helping the Sisters, I'm sure they couldn't do it all on there own?" I was fishing for anything, any clues at all.

"I never knew anybody to work in the Convent only the Sisters" said Mary then she said.

"Do you mind the yarn went round one time about the young lassie that was left at the door and the Mother took her in? Whatever happened that time I mind there was a whole hoo haa but I can't mind the right way of it now?"

Mary rubbed her forehead, "Do you mind that Aggie?" she asked Nana but Nana said,

"I never heard that, I doubt you're doting Mary." Mary moved to the edge of her seat.

"Indeed I'm not doting I mind it well, sure we used to have an old chest of drawers and my Mother, God rest her soul, used to put ol newspapers in the bottom of the drawers and I mind reading about it months after the whole thing died down, it was in the paper in the drawers, do you mind it Elsa?" she asked.

"I mind something like that but I couldn't tell the right road of it now Mary."

Winnie said, "I don't mind that either Mary," but Mary replied,

"Och it was only a few years after you moved up here."

I thought to myself this is a debate that could last the rest of the evening so I made my excuses and went home. Next day at school I told the girls what I had found out and the fact that Ellen's story might be the truth, because one of the old ladies at Nana's sheltered housing had mentioned she knew something strange went on up a the Convent with a young woman who was left there. Claire started, "That's not a pile of good to us is it, one old lady remembers something?"

Madonna and Niamh agreed. "Hang on girls, Mary, the old lady said she saw it in the paper as well, and if it was in the newspaper then we can look it up in old copies, right?" I explained.

"Aye she's right; they got them in the library. My brother Luke used to look up old Dubliners stuff about Luke Kelly the guy he was named after. The woman is really helpful. I was with him one time and she got him all he wanted to find. My brother couldn't his own bum in the dark but got all he needed, we should go and check it out," Niamh said, so after school we headed for the library. Madonna was a member and asked, "Is it possible to look up old newspaper stories?" the lady at the front desk showed us to a thing that looked like a projector but explained that we weren't allowed to use it; it had to be one of the staff. A few minutes later and an oldish lady arrived with half moon glasses.

"Can I help you girls?" she said.

"Yes, well we hope so. We are from the Convent and we're doing a history project on the Convent and we were hoping there might be some old newspaper stories we could use?" I said very confidently.

"That's very interesting, what kind of stuff are you looking for?" she replied.

"Well we are each doing a different era and I got 1950 until 1955. Have you got anything in that era?" said Niamh quickly. She was proving to be very bright and quick.

"That makes it a bit easier, let's try the Gazette," said the lady firing up this machine and going to work. "Ah here we are," she said, "1950, and the new Mother Superior is elected at the St Frances Convent Rosnarene. There's a picture of the new Mother, I mind her," said the lady pointing at a picture on a screen then she went on, "The crater only lasted about six or seven years and then she passed away. The Nun to her right in the picture is the Mother up there now; you girls would know her wouldn't you?"

We had a look, and although it was nearly thirty five years ago we could recognise the Mother Superior now. "Is there any other stories missus, anything about the building or anything like that?" asked Claire.

"Em, let me see, there is a wee bit there on a model of the Convent being unveiled in the parochial hall in '52, it has Ronnie and May Carson presenting the Sisters of St Frances Convent with a model of the school made solely from local materials. Also pictured are Dennis Hamilton and Rory Gervin who also constructed the model."

The library lady was very helpful. "Is that story any good for you girls, though I have no idea what ever happened to that model," she said looking at us again.

"It's very interesting isn't it?" Niamh added.

"There's another bit there from 1954 but that's in the legal section and use are still minors so you're not allowed that information I'm afraid, but surely you have enough to keep you going there eh?" said the lady shutting down the machine.

"Yeah that's been a great help. Thank you. We'll go and get started, thanks again. Bye!"

We went back up to the park and sat and tried to think of a way to get Ellen back into the public eye or to try and find out what happened. We were huddled in the corner of the park working on our next move when we heard; "Hello ladies, are you playing spin the bottle?"

It had to be Mickey Thompson.

"You're supposed to have a boy or two when you play spin the bottle," he said.

"C'mon Mickey and you can play with us, I hope they pick us two Mickey," said Niamh smiling at poor Mickey.

"You stay where you're at over there, I can understand why you can't take your eyes off me but I have to tell you I'm spoken for already so you may look elsewhere," he said puffing out his budgie like chest. Claire just burst out in fits of laughter;

"Spoken for? By whom?" she roared.

"That is none of your business two tonne Tessie!" Mickey said in bad temper, but Claire had lost her cool this time.

"That's it you wee nerd I'm going to kick the ..."

Claire didn't get finishing that line as her Mum came into the park with Paula, Claire's wee sister.

"Is she alright with you there for a bit, I've a stack of ironing to do and she wants a bit of fresh air, she's been cooped up in that house all day," her Mum said leading wee Paula down towards us.

"Aye she's grand here with me and the girls," said Claire.

"Your Dad was to be home by now from the town but he hasn't appeared. He's disappeared off the face of the earth, he's the new Ellen Daly!" she said.

"Who?" asked Claire?

"Ahh you wouldn't know her, before your time love. I'll call you nearer dinner time, be careful and watch that young one," said her Mum as she went back out of the park.

"Ellen Daly, do you think?" I was about to ask, but Madonna interrupted;

"It must be, it has to be, that's too much of a coincidence," Niamh said, "Claire you're going to have to quiz your Mum and see what she knows, she has obviously heard something somewhere."

Mickey piped up, "What about, who's Helen whatever you said?" he asked but nobody answered him. We had some leads but a lot of loose ends to try and connect. The ball was in Claire's court now she was going to chat to her Mum and fingers crossed tomorrow when we go down to see Ellen we'll at least have some information on her or who knows maybe something to tell her.

We met in the park early on Saturday but Claire couldn't shed much light on Ellen. She said she had asked her Mum but she just said it was an old saying years ago around the Grange and Rosnarene that if anybody took a long time doing something or if they were away a long time, people would say "You're the new Ellen Daly." She said it must have been after somebody called Ellen Daly who went somewhere and never came back but Claire's Mum didn't know if she was real or not. We went back down the usual track making sure that nobody followed and soon arrived back at Ellen's little hut. "Hello! Ellen are you there?" I asked but there was no reply, I tried again "Ellen, hello!" still nothing "She must have gone somewhere, there's no dog or anything, but she didn't go far as the clothes and food stuff are still here," said Madonna poking her head through the open doorway. We had a stroll around and checked about for Ellen but there was no sign of her. After about a half hour and with us getting ready to leave Ellen came through the trees. She was lugging a coal bag on her back. "Hey Ellen, do you want some help with that?" asked Claire.

"Nah child, I'm alright with this," she said taking it straight into the hovel. "What brings you lot down here today?" she continued closing the makeshift door and keeping us outside.

"We just thought as it's the weekend we'd pop down and see if you want or need anything?" I asked.

"We were doing some research on you as well, and looking up old stories of the Convent in the past," said Claire.

Ellen was furious, "What did tell you when I first met you, you were to tell no-one I was here, and I meant no-one. This could mean trouble for me. I trusted you lot and you let me down so go, go now and don't come back!"

I tried to explain, "We didn't tell anyone, we were just trying to help and get the truth, and nobody knows you're here."

But Ellen was adamant; "Get away from here and don't come back or I'll set the dog on you, go on!" she shouted going inside and closing the door.

"Nice one Claire," said Niamh.

"Shut it or I'll box your ears Niamh, I was only trying to explain we were going to get to know her," Claire came back.

"Hang on, Hang on" said Madonna. "Give over you two," she spoke a little louder, "You have annoyed Miss Daly now so let's just leave her in peace."

The door of the hovel trailed opened.

"How did you know that?" asked Ellen.

"Know what?" asked Madonna.

"The Daly part, how did you know my second name was Daly?" Ellen asked.

"Well up in the Grange and Rosnarene they talk about being away as long as Ellen Daly and we thought that might be you? Is it?" enquired Madonna.

"I'm the joke up there now am I? I don't care. I know the truth and someday so will they," Ellen said closing the door over.

"Wait!" I shouted, "Please Ellen let us help you, we can do things up in the town that can help you, we can help get the truth out and we won't reveal where you are I promise, we all do."

Ellen looked long and hard at me and the others.

"It's probably too late for the truth now but it would be nice to clear my name and be able to live a proper normal life again," she said looking up to the sky. "Agh it's too late for that," she continued. "Well at least let us try, eh? What have you got to loose Ellen?" said Niamh.

Ellen laughed, "My mansion and all it's grandeur!" She shook her head, "If you want to try and help then go ahead but not a word about where I am," she said. "C'mon in here and sit down and I'll tell you what you should do."

Ellen opened the coal bag and took out a frozen chicken.

"Where the heck did you get that Ellen, were you shopping?" I asked.

"Aye you could say that, anyway when you go up there again you need to find Gertie Gates if she's still around. I used to be friendly with her and although she had to side with the towns people she knew I was the victim so she can help you most around the village. I never got the name of the lady who paid me to steal from the Convent. Gertie might know her though?" she said as Madonna was writing down the details.

"Do you mind me asking how much you were paid; I mean was it a lot? If it was then we know we're looking for somebody who is rich?" said Niamh.

"Sure you know what I was paid, I gave you the coins. I got twelve gold coins and the lady told me they are worth more than any money in Ireland. I gave you one each didn't you exchange them yet?" Ellen asked.

"That's another clue we could check out," suggested Claire.

"I have the other eight here in the purse, and I will return them to the lady who gave them to me, they ruined my whole life and so did she."

Ellen was getting a bit upset so we figured we would go and let her have some space. As we left, Ellen emptied out the rest of the coal bag which contained a couple of blocks of wood some old magazine and papers and about one good shovel full of coal.

When we got back up into the park we went to Claire's uncles house, he was the man that had said the coins were possibly French but wasn't sure. He invited us in and Claire produced the coin again; "What do you think it is Uncle Hugh?" she asked.

"I think it definitely is French, it has a Cockerel on it which tells me France. It's dated 1924, which could mean it might have some value but it doesn't have a royal marking or stamp of any kind and that unfortunately tells me it's a fake coin," he said.

"A fake? How do you mean Hugh, is it not real money or is it just no worth anything now?" Claire asked as we looked on.

"Without a royal mint marking or a royal seal or stamp it means that the coin isn't a real coin. It's like Monopoly money these days, you might find if you scratch the coin really hard with something sharp the gold will scratch off to leave a tin or slate underneath. It's a toy I'm afraid," he said.

"Its useless then?" asked Madonna.

"Yeah I'm afraid you won't buy many sweets with that," he said handing it back to Claire. We thanked him for his time and left feeling even more dejected than ever, it seemed every time we got a good lead it fell flat on its face.

"I bet Gertie Gates is dead too," said Niamh, sighing.

"Probably," agreed Claire.

"C'mon guys we said we would help Ellen and we can't just stop at every set back?" I said. "Some of our Mums or Dads are bound to know who Gertie Gates is or was and then we can get our investigation going again," I said.

"Bowlhead is right, we should all ask at home and see if we can find this Gertie Gates and be back at the park tomorrow with any leads," said Claire and we each went home a little more hopeful.

I arrived back at the house and Trina, Pauric and Whitney were over visiting. Dad was in the bookies with Kieran and Mum was making the dinner.

"Hi everybody, hello wee woman," I said picking up Whitney as I came in.

"Hello Billy," said Trina.

"Any word on the mystery woman?" asked Pauric sniggering.

"Nah there's no mystery woman Pauric. Unless of course you know any?" I snapped back.

Mum came in from the kitchen, "The rover returns, where have you been from morning?" she asked.

"Just up in the park and out for a wee walk with the girls. Why did you miss me?" I replied.

"Like a hole in the head," said Mum smugly.

"Hi Mum do you know Gertie Gates?" I asked.

"Who? Gertie Gates? I knew the Gates used to live in the big house just at the bus stop but they moved out before you were born, I can't say I know Gertie Gates," she said.

"My Mum was Gertie Gates before she married my Dad," said Pauric, "she was Gates to her own name, to be fair she didn't like being called Gertie because my Granny called her Gertrude and said that's your name."

I could hardly contain the excitement! "Was she really, and how old would your Mum be, roughly like?" I asked.

"She'd only have been turning 60 had she have been here to see it," he said.

I remembered then that Paurics Mum had passed away and so had my short lived excitement. I never got to the park on Sunday to meet up with the girls as Mum had suggested we all take a lovely walk on Sunday afternoon. We took Nana along too and it was a sunny day. We went up by the Mill Hill and met the Thompson family out for a walk too, Mr Thompson, linking onto his wife with Colin and Mickey close behind all dressed up in their Sunday bests. I was pushing Whitney and was a little way behind so Mr and Mrs Thompson stopped to admire the baby.

"How old is this wee lady then?" asked Mrs Thompson.

"I think she's coming one and a bit," I answered.

"Look at the wee chubby cheeks on her, that's the way you looked Michael when you were a baby," said Mrs Thompson pointing at Whitney and looking at Mickey. Mickey's' face was going red;

"You don't need to tell the whole world my life story Mum," he said as he pushed past.

"Nice tank top Mickey," I whispered.

"Belt up pin head," he snarled.

"I'd better go and catch up," I said to the Thompson parents as Whitney and I gave chase to Mum, Nana, Trina and Pauric. We took a break at the summer seat so Nana could recharge the batteries and started; "Did you bring a picnic? I love a wee picnic, just sit on the grass in the sunshine and enjoy a wee snack." She looked at Mum.

"I have a bottle of Lucozade in my bag if that's any good to you?" Mum said and Trina joined in giggling; "Whitney has a couple of Farley Rusk's with her?"

Nana wasn't amused, "You're all very funny today, I hope it's not catching," she said sarcastically. "I was going to make a round of sandwiches myself but I couldn't," said Nana.

"Why Ma had you no bread or butter?" asked Mum.

"I have any amount of bread and butter thank you, but the wee chicken I bought took legs and walked!" Nana folded her arms. "I'm keeping a very close eye on Mary next door; I think that's where it went. The next thing I set out, I'll put a taste of something on it and she'll be on the porcelain for a day or two," she said nodding her head.

"Why would Mary want to take your chicken, are you sure you even had a chicken?" asked Trina. "Do you think I'm going doo lally? Of course I had a blooming chicken. I took it out of the freezer and it was as hard as a goats knee so I sat it out on the bunker in the sunshine to thaw out a bit and when I went back out it was away."

Trina and Mum were in stitches laughing but Nana wasn't best pleased.

"Aye laugh away there, I hope whoever took it has the diarrhoea for a fortnight," she said.

I thought I knew where the chicken had gone, but how did Ellen get up from the woods to Nanas flat at the sheltered housing without anybody seeing her? On our way home from the walk I called in at Claire's as Mum, Nana, Trina, Pauric and Whitney all went back to our place.

"Hi Claire, how did you get on today down at Ellen's?" I asked.

"We didn't go down today, you were away, Niamh was at her Aunties and Madonna didn't want to be coming over on her own so we just thought we'll leave it to next week. Any word on Gertie Gates?" she asked.

"Yes and No, my Mum said there used to be Gates that lived down near the bus stop but they moved and Trina's husband Pauric, his Ma was called Gertie Gates but she died. What about you?" I said hopefully.

"Same here my Mum knew the Gates' that lived in the big house down the road but she said there was none of them Gertie that she knew," Claire replied.

We were back at another dead end. "Maybe Niamh or Madonna had better luck," I suggested but Claire shook her head, "Nah Niamh and Madonna had no luck either I asked them earlier."

It was late in the day to go down to visit Ellen so we decided we'd just go up into the park. We were only in the park five minutes when Mickey came in on the bike. I thought I'd wind him up:

"Hello wee chubby cheeks," I said laughing.

"Claire, pinhead is talking to you," Mickey said as he circled round.

"His Mummy was telling me all about him earlier when we were out walking. He was the cutest wee baby in the world with chubby cheeks," I explained to Claire as she looked confused.

"Shut up, you're a mouth pin head; my Ma was just making pleasant talk to pass herself. She got me mixed up with Colin anyway."

Mickey said trying to wriggle out of the embarrassment.

"She seemed pretty sure who she meant when she was talking to me, and that's what she said," I winked at Claire. "Niamh will be even madder about you now baby face!" I shouted.

"Shut up pin head," he said then started on Claire;

"I hear your wee sister is learning to count using your chins, she can count up till three!"

Mickey was laughing and didn't see Claire run towards him and before he knew where he was she slapped him on the back of the neck. Mickey jolted and the bike careered down the slope with Mickey's legs sticking out each side like he was doing the splits.

"Pull your brakes!" I shouted but he just kept going building up speed. Crash! Into the See Saw he went, his bike stopping instantly but Mickey flying through the air like a trapeze artist, he disappeared out of sight behind the See Saw then we heard "Waaaaaa!!!!!!!!!!"

then a break, then "Waaaaaaaa!!!!!!!!!"

Mickey rose up from behind the See Saw, his tank top covered in dog mess, he had a scratch on his fore head but apart from that no obvious injury.

"Waaaaaaaaaaa!" he went again.

"Och give over will you, you only fell off your bike," Claire said shaking her head. Mickey gathered up the bike and the front wheel was buckled out of shape, as he tried to push it past us it made an awful sound like somebody trailing a heavy chest along the ground.

"You're dead, you big fat horse," Mickey sniffled through the tears as he limped past.

"Do you want another slap?" Claire asked jumping off the roundabout.

"Waaaaaa leave me alone!" Mickey screamed as everybody in the park turned round. I was embarrassed more than Mickey now. "C'mon Claire let's get out of here before they send for the Police," I said.

"I done nothing, I only gave him a tap, if he can't ride his bike that's his fault!" she said turning towards home. "See you tomorrow Billy Bowl head," she shouted laughing.

"That's if you're allowed when your Mum hears from the Thompsons," I replied.

"Oooh I'm scared now" Claire shouted as she went out of sight up home. Mickey disappeared in the other direction with the busted bicycle.

Chapter 11

The next few days were the normal schedule around Rosnarene, me and the girls going to St Frances' during the day and trying to be Charlie's Angels and solve the mystery of Ellen Daly the rest of the time. On Friday evening Claire and I were in Rosnarene and had planned to go to the pictures when we met Baz, Colin and Mickey.

"Hi girls are you for the flicks?" asked Baz.

"Aye we we're hoping to head that road, what are you dudes up to?" Claire said.

"We're going to Luke Cosgrove's birthday; he's 16 tomorrow so we're just going to hang out and maybe go to the Cinema too, what's on?" asked Colin.

"A Nightmare on Elm Street," said Claire. She went on, "it's about this man with knives in a glove and if you fall asleep he'll come and kill you. Something like that anyway."

Baz and Colin looked interested. "That child won't get into that," Claire said pointing at Mickey. "Shut your mouth will ya and go and mind your own business. You'll have to pay for two seats in the pictures any way," Mickey replied.

"That's very original Mickey, a joke about Claire being heavy, when will you change the record?" I said.

"You shut up as well fart face. Away back to sleep for another couple of months and we'll all get a bit of peace," he shouted. Colin and Baz just sniggered;

"Something funny lads?" I asked.

"Nah it's just Mickey can wind you girls up so easy, fart face, sponge face, pin head," they laughed. "Where does he get them from?" said Baz.

"Well none of his wit or bad manners comes from his parents anyway, they're dead on people. I met them before and they're really nice." I confirmed.

"I know that I've been in their house and Mickey is very different at home too," said Baz.

"Don't you start mouthing on next Baz, you come around our place and slobber on about all the new gadgets and things you get," Mickey said puling a funny face; "I've got a digital watch, I've got he new Atari TV game, I've got, I've got, I've got that's all you say, you give me the willies listening to you!" Baz was a bit cross.

"At least I'm not a Mummy's boy like you!" he said.

"Nah you're a Mummy's and Daddy's boy, you get everything you want. You're Cassie and Eamon's wee soldier aren't you? You should get a dress on you!" Mickey said dancing around pulling the bottom of his jumper to make it look like a dress; "Look I'm Barry Corke la le la," he shouted, but Barry was very angry. Colin calmed the situation down a bit;

"Give over the both of you, you're worse than two old women," he said as Claire and I just laughed. Luke arrived and the boys headed off to the cafe with Baz

181

and Mickey at opposite sides of the foursome, casting dirty glances at each other every two seconds. We went on to the Cinema, but didn't see the boys after that. I have to say after ninety five minutes of Freddy Kruger I was ready for home, making sure to check under the bed and hoping I don't wake up dead after a visit during the night from the pointy fingered freak.

On the Saturday I was getting ready to go up to meet Claire and the others when there was a knock at the door. I was in the kitchen when Cassie and Eamon came in, Mum was leading the way.

"That's awful Cassie, when did he do that? The dirty wee devil," Mum said.

"Last night, they were all down the town for some lad's birthday and they were to go to the pictures and seemingly this is where the whole thing kicked off," Cassie explained.

"What's happened?"

I didn't really care but was just being nosey. Cassie said;

"Barry and the two Thompson lads went into town last night to go to the Cinema. They were to meet young Cosgrove because it was his birthday or something; anyway they went to see some film and young Mickey Thompson wasn't getting in so they decided they'd g up to the wee cafe instead. Whatever happened up there Mickey and our Barry fell out and young Thompson threw a cup of mineral over Barry and Barry give a clout." She stopped and took a drag of the fag then continued, "Young Thompson started roaring and shouting and the young girl put him out and things settled down between the bigger boys, although Barry's' shirt and vest were soaking. After a while Barry, the bigger lad Thompson and young Cosgrove came out and were sitting against the wall waiting on young Cosgrove's lift."

I knew by Cassie's face something bad was going to happen and I couldn't wait;

"What happened then?" I asked.

"Well do you mind young Thompson who was put out earlier, well if he didn't climb up on the wall and wee down on top of Barry, I mean what kind of an animal is he?" she asked while my Mum covered her mouth from laughing out loud.

"Then what?" I asked.

"If that wasn't bad enough he shouted at our Barry do you want some shampoo? I think that young fella needs looked at," said Cassie, then Eamon joined in;

"I wouldn't be surprised if Barry doesn't end up with something, it can't be very hygienic that?"

I wanted to laugh but I knew they'd be furious so I said; "They were arguing earlier when Claire and I met them, Mickey Thompson doesn't know what to be at. The difference between him and Colin is like day and night," I continued, "What are you going to do about it?" Mum asked.

"I'm going down to the paper shop where his Mother works and I'll let her know what kind of a boy she's bringing up, it's a disgrace isn't it. You can't go round peeing on people!"

Cassie sighed and said; "I know the Mother, I met her one time at the weight watchers, she works part time in Kelly's paper shop in the village. Do you know her Imelda?" she asked Mum.

"I never be in there to be honest Cassie, Tommy might know her though he gets the paper in there every morning and studies the horses," Mum said with a smirk.

"Then he will know her alright, she's always a great word for the men, we used to call her Flirty Gertie at the weight watchers," said Cassie. Mum made a cup of tea and they went into the living room and I went on out and up to the park to the usual rendezvous point with the girls. I met Colin and I said; "I hear your Mickey is in bother with my Auntie Cassie, she's down in our house and she's going to chat to your Ma?"

Colin nodded, "Aye my Da has already grounded him, and you wouldn't believe what he did."

I interrupted, "I heard already, thanks," but Colin went on, "Da says he gets it from Mums side of the family, my Mums brother Gusty was an absolute looper, he'd have done anything for a laugh or a bet?" he said.

"I never heard of him, is he in the Grange?" I asked.

"Nah, my Mums clan are from up the country, she moved down here with her Mum to seek her fortune and ended up she met my Da, must have been the booby prize. Gusty is a legend, he's famous up there, everybody knows Gusty Gates, mind you he must be sixty now," Colin explained. "Well there's a new Gusty now known as Mickey the legend, I'll see you later Collie," I said and went on into the park. After we exchanged the pleasantries we got down to the case at hand. We chatted for a while exploring different avenues when suddenly the penny dropped with a big clunk inside my head:

"I know who she is!" I shouted.

"What?" asked Niamh?

"I know who Gertie Gates is, it's staring me in the face the whole time, its flirty Gertie!" I said looking at the others as they stared back with blank expressions.

"My Auntie is going to complain to Mickey Thompsons Ma because he peed on Baz's' head last night, but Mickey takes he's crazy streak after his mad uncle Gusty, don't you see Gusty Gates is Gertie Thompson's brother and before she was married she was Gertie Gates!"

The girls just stood there with their mouths wide open.

"What are you on Bowl head? Did you fall again walking up here?" asked Claire.

"No, look I know I'm right. C'mon we have to go to Kelly's newsagents in the town, that's where Ellen's friend is, I will explain on the way."

I started off and the girls followed as I explained in more detail what I had picked up from listening to Cassie and from chatting to Colin. We soon arrived at the shop and when we went in a lady stood behind the counter, though you couldn't see the counter for newspapers and magazines.

"Hello girls, what can I do for you?" she asked.

"We are looking for someone and we hoped you could help us?" Madonna said.

"If I can," replied the lady.

"Are you Gertie?" Madonna just blurted straight out.

"Well who wants to know?" she said smiling.

"We do, we are trying to find a lady who works here and she is called Gertie, is that you?" Niamh asked.

"I thought you were going to say a handsome knight on a big White Stallion was coming to sweep me off my feet and take me away to never, never land but seeing as that's not going to happen, yeah I'm Gertie so what do you want with me then?" she said.

"We are trying to help a friend and we were asked to try and find a lady called Gertie Gates," I said and paused for a reply.

"Jeepers you're going back a bit now, I haven't been called Gertie Gates since Lassie was a pup, who told you about Gertie Gates? Is this a wind up?" said the lady.

"No, it's very important but you have to promise to keep it a secret," said Claire as I continued;

"I had a bad fall up by Green water and I was very badly hurt but it could have been worse only for a lady helping me, that lady was Ellen Daly."

I didn't have to say anymore as the fun smiley expression on Gerties face changed instantly.

"Ellen Daly," she said, "You must have made a mistake surely, it couldn't be Ellen Daly, no not possible." she sat down.

"It was Ellen Daly and she asked us to try and find you, but she called you Gates not Thompson," Niamh asked.

"Aye well when I knew Ellen there was no Mr Thompson so I was Gates, there was just me and Mummy who moved down here and I knew nobody. One evening I was up at the Convent looking about a wee part time job. I was finishing school and things were a bit tight. I met Ellen because she lived up there, och now she was a few years older than me but we got talking and became quite good pals. We would take the odd day window shopping but we had no money to buy anything and then Ellen appeared to come into money just out of the blue and it wasn't long after that she was a goner."

Gertie was a little teary eyed; "I only spoke to her once after that and although she was doing what she thought was best she was labelled, and my Mother forbid me to be anywhere near her, it was a real pity because she was so innocent but that's a long time ago, God knows where she is now?" Gertie said getting up to sell papers to a man who had came into the shop. After the man had left I asked Gertie, "If Ellen was still knocking about now would you help us to help her?" she smiled.

"If is a big word child."

Madonna stepped forward; "We know where Ellen is Mrs Thompson, we talk to her regularly and she does need our help. Will you help us?" Madonna asked.

"Can I speak to her then?" Gertie said.

"We will have to ask her first, she doesn't trust anybody and was cross when she thought we had told people in the town where she was." Madonna paused,

"It's probably ok but we need to ask Ellen's permission."

Gertie leaned on the counter, "You said you talked to her, and then you said you know where she is, is she here in Rosnarene?" she asked.

"We can't tell you that yet, maybe we cold meet up and chat to you sometime when you're not at work?" I suggested.

"Surely, pop round the house this afternoon and I'll tell you what I know. Ellen Daly after all these years," she said shaking her head. We agreed to call at Thompson's house later and left as the shop was getting a bit busy. After the paper shop we went straight to the park and on down the steep steps to the woods. We made our way to Ellen's tin shack and she was just a few yards away gathering sticks and firewood.

"Hi ya Ellen, how are you this week?" Niamh shouted.

"My God, that's a big noise from such a small girl. You gave me a fright there. How are you girls?" Ellen said.

"We are great Ellen and we have got some good news for you. We have found Gertie Gates!" I announced all chuffed with myself.

"Did you find her? Does she remember me? What did she say?" Ellen appeared excited.

"Yep she remembers you alright, she told us about you being mates and she wants to talk to you? I explained.

"No!" Ellen snapped.

"But she is willing to help us. I think she still doesn't believe us that we know you and where you are. We have nothing to convince her, no proof of anything?" Claire said.

Ellen glared at us and went into the hovel, in a few seconds she appeared in the doorway with the small suitcase. "Here take this and give it to Gertie," she said holding out a picture of two young girls. They were very pretty and after studying the picture in more detail it was clear the two girls in the picture were in fact Ellen and Gertie.

"I'm going to get a few things so you'll have to make yourselves scarce," Ellen said shutting the old door of the shack.

"We have to go and meet Gertie in the afternoon anyway so we'll call tomorrow and let you know what we found out," I said but Ellen just walked off nodding.

"Girls I'll meet you up in the village in about an hour or so I got something I need to do," I said, as I ran into the cave opening and up the steps.

"Billy what's the rush?" Claire shouted.

"I'll tell you later, got to go," I replied. Once out at the top I ran across the embankment and through the park. Out onto the road and a sharp right had me in line for home but I wasn't going home. At the top of the lane I waited and the bus arrived, "One to Rosnarene," I said and took my seat bus ticket in hand. A few minutes later I was off the bus again and running like my life depended on it. Up the Convent lane, round the back of St Frances' and down the short hill to the sheltered housing and stopped out of breath at number

189

2. I pressed the buzzer but no answer, I pressed again but still nothing.

"They're away into town love," shouted Winnie from across the way.

"They went about an hour ago, do you want to come in here and wait?" she asked.

"Nah I'm ok thank you, who went with Nana?"

I asked Winnie because she never missed anything out her window.

"Aggie and Mary are away in a taxi," she said.

"Oh right, that's great thanks Winnie," I said and watched as she disappeared back into her own flat then I scooted around the back of Nana's. Nana had a small garden at the back with a hedgerow at the bottom. I had a quick look round and a look into Mary's garden next door it was the same, just the coal bunker and a couple bags of blocks. I sat in behind the bunker and waited and after about twenty minutes I heard a rustling in the hedgerow and there was Ellen, poking her head through a gap in the bush. I watched as she made her way up to Mary's bunker next door and started to fill her coal bag with handfuls of coal and the odd block or two. In a few seconds she was back down the garden and through the small hole in the hedge and out of sight. I waited and then followed her down the garden and through the same hole; on the other side of the hedge was a field of tall grass and a steep slope down to an overgrown pathway which lead back into the woods. Ellen was able to pass through the forest and out the opposite side to the Green water and park and up through the field and come out at the sheltered housing, or go on up the field and arrive at the back of the Convent. I remembered her saying: "I've been up there a few times and had a look at the Nuns but they didn't know I was there," and this is how she must have done it. My detective skills were getting better, but now I had to get back to the bus stop and back into the Grange to meet up with the girls and then to go to see Gertie. I was going to be wrecked but things were slowly taking shape.

I arrived back in the Grange in time and met up with the rest of my intrepid detectives;

"Where did you go?" asked Claire.

"I'll tell you later, I've got something to show you lot later on too," I said. We made our way down towards the Thompson house and Mickey was in the front garden raking up the fresh cut grass; "Hello gorgeous!" shouted Niamh but Mickey just gave us a dirty look.

"What's up with you, you've a face like a slapped bum," said Claire laughing.

"You've got a face just like a bum," Mickey snapped back.

"Have you that grass done yet?" his Mum shouted from the doorway, "When you have it raked up, get it in a bag and get it dumped. Then come in and I'll give you something else to do!"

Mickey's Mum sounded cross; "Are you in trouble Mickey?" asked Niamh.

"Aye, I threw water over pretty boy Corke at the flicks last night and he went and told his Ma, he's such a big girl's blouse," Mickey replied.

"You're a lying wee toe rag, you did more than throw water, Cassie told my Mum you peed on Baz," I said.

"You dirty wee devil," Claire joined in, and then Madonna;

"That's disgusting, it's sick" she said.

"I did not, I got a mineral bottle and filled with the drain water and poured down on top of them when they were at the wall. Your Luke started shouting watch out he's peeing and that's where the whole lies started," Mickey said looking at Niamh, then he turned to me;

"Your squad are all the same, drama queens, like you when you fell and started the whole story of the magic woman, your family are full of bull sh.."

"Michael!" roared Mickey's Mum, "Get in here now and wash your mouth out, that week of no pocket money is now a fortnight. You'll learn manners one way or another boyo!"

Mickey slumped over the rake and then slammed it into the ground and trudged off towards the house.

"Happy now, pin head," he said under his breath as he passed by us.

"C'mon in girls, and I'm sorry for any back cheek you got from this one," Mrs Thompson said as she opened the front door wide to let Mickey in past her. We went in and she showed us through to the kitchen, there was a big wooden table with 6 chairs and glasses of lemonade,

"Help yourselves there," said Mrs Thompson as she sat down at the head of the table. We had a glass each and sat down.

"Right let's get cracking then," said Mrs Thompson, "What do you want to know?" she asked.

"Well we met Ellen Daly and she told us to find you, as you were her friend and she gave us this to show you for proof," I said presenting the picture. Mrs Thompson studied the picture;

"My Lord, this was taken at the fete in the village many moons ago, me and Ellen had only known each other a wee while and we got our picture took for the paper. It was near my time for leaving school and Ellen would have been oh about nineteen or twenty," she smiled. "Ellen kept this all this time eh, my, my," she sighed.

"Yeah she has a suitcase and who knows what else is in it," said Claire.

"What can you tell us about the gold coins Mrs Thompson?" Madonna asked.

"Please call me Gertie," she said and then went on.

"Ellen told me that she was doing a wee job for a lady who had asked her to get something from the convent. I thought she meant holy water or something like that, anyway it turns out the lady wanted something that belonged to the Convent so when Ellen took it to her she got paid with these coins." Gertie filled up our glasses and then continued, "A few days after that the whole town was talking about the thief that stole from the Sister's up at St Frances. It was a big crime in them days to take from the Nuns and poor Ellen was frowned upon by everybody, even my Mother said I shouldn't be seen talking to her."

Gertie was visibly annoyed, "I went to the Convent to tell Ellen what my Mum had said but she had gone, the Mother had cast her out and told her when she was repentant she could return with the missing item and seek forgiveness. Ellen went in search of the lady to get the item back but the lady refused and said she knew nothing. Ellen was devastated and everyone in town wanted her out, and a couple of days later Ellen was gone and I never seen or heard from her since."

Gertie just sat there staring then turned to us.

"So what way can I help you kids then, I've told you all I know or remember", she said.

"Do you know who the lady was that she took the item for or what was it she took?" asked Niamh.

"I never saw the lady she stole for but I remember the item was a piece from the sculpture of St Frances, it was a mosaic thing of the school that used to be on show in the town and then it was brought up to the school. It really was wonderful work and beautiful to look at when it was complete but it was worthless with a piece missing. It was like a jigsaw with a bit missing," Mrs Thompson explained.

"Where is the piece now?" asked Madonna.

"That's the million dollar question; whoever has the piece has the missing link to the whole story. Only they know the whole truth, and probably only they can prove Ellen is innocent." Gertie looked around us individually:

"If you find the piece, you'll solve the problem."

This was getting like a real Charlie's Angels case now, but where would we even start to look, is there anybody we can turn to?

"Have you any idea where we should start to look Gertie?" I asked.

"I haven't a clue; most of the ladies from them days are dead and gone or up in the nursing home. Unless some of the older generation can help you?" She boiled the kettle. "I'll make a cuppa and you tell me about Ellen now."

Mrs Thompson brought out the sandwiches and we talked about my fall and about how we actually found Ellen. We could trust Gertie, we knew that, but during the tea Mickey and Colin came into the kitchen and sat down;

"What's all this?" asked Colin. His Mum replied;

"These young ladies know an old fiend of mine and we were just sharing some memories, have you that grass lifted and dumped yet?" she growled at Mickey,

"Yes, it's dumped and after my tea I'll trim under the trees with a pair of scissors, or clean the slabs with a tooth brush," Mickey said sarcastically.

"You'll be in your bed if you keep talking mister smarty pants," his Mother replied.

"How would these girls know an old friend of yours, they're only kids?" Colin queried.

"It's a long story, any more tea girls?" she asked.

"No thank you," I said, "I'm full up, the tea was lovely and thanks for the sandwiches, that cheese was beautiful, did you get it in town?" I asked.

"Nah we stole it from a mouse trap," said Mickey.

"Right that's your lot Michael!" Mrs Thompson grabbed Mickey by the ear and nearly lifted him off the ground. "You're hurting me!" he shouted.

"Yep, that's the plan," she said opening the door that led into the hallway. "Now away you go to your room, you can come back down when you learn a bit of manners."

She apologised to us and started to clear away the dishes, we thanked her for her help and the tea and left to go back up to the park and put our heads together to see what we could do next.

We chatted for hours and couldn't come up with a single way to find the missing piece of the sculpture, we couldn't even think of a place to start to look. We agreed to sleep on it and see what we might come up with on the Sunday but unfortunately the Sunday came and went and although we went down and told Ellen all about Gertie and what she had to say, we still couldn't think of any way of finding the missing piece. We continued visiting Ellen and asking around but our case was dead in the water. Ellen still was very independent and wouldn't directly accept any help from us but we were able to play her at that game. Anything we wanted her to have like a new cardigan or some decent food we would leave outside Nana or Marys back garden and funnily enough a day or two later it would magically appear in Ellen's little shack.

The summer came around and we broke off school but still kept meeting up each weekend and visiting Ellen. On one of the sunnier days I went up to Nana's to see if there was anything she needed doing. I got the bus up to Rosnarene and went around the convent to the sheltered housing, after pressing the buzzer at Nana's flat for ages and getting no reply I thought there must be something wrong. What made it even more suspicious was the fact that nosey Winnie hadn't appeared from across the street to see what was going on. I went next door to Mary's flat and again the answer was the same, I buzzed the door but no reply. I even tried Elsa's flat but there was no life about there either. I wondered where they all could have went to when I heard music playing so I went around the back of Mary's flat and there they all were in swimming costumes and sun glasses. Nana and Mary were sitting on two white plastic chairs while Elsa was spread out on a blanket. Winnie was sitting on a lilo which was only three quarter way blown up and each time she moved it sounded like somebody breaking wind.

"What are you lot doing?" I asked.

"We were talking earlier and found that none of us had been to the beach in years so we are having a beach party," said Winnie.

"In Mary's back garden? No sand or water, it's some beach!" I started laughing.

"You have to make do," shouted Elsa from the blanket. "Use your imagination; we've got lovely sunshine, our swimming cosies on and a lilo. We've also had a couple of beach cocktails and music," she continued.

"God help us they're on the drink, as if they are not bad enough sober!" I said loudly.

"What do you want anyway?" asked Nana.

"That's gratitude for you eh? I called to see did you want anything from the town and that's the thanks I get!" I replied.

"It's funny you should ask, I need one of them muscle rubs for my bad back," said Nana.

"You don't have a bad back Nana," I said.

"I do now, I hurt it in the final of the limbo competition an hour ago!" She busted out laughing and the others joined in. I had obviously been set up with the back rub story.

"Oh very good, very funny, I wonder what Sister Bridget will say when she hears about the drinking going on?"

I threatened to tell but they didn't care much, the Beach boys Surfing USA was playing and Winnie was standing on the lilo rocking back and forth and pretending to surf while farting noises had the other three in fits of laughter. It was pointless trying to get any sense out of this lot until they were a little less intoxicated. I went up to the Convent and had a wee chat with Sister Bridget as she was out doing a bit of work in the gardens. I asked could I go and see the Mosaic again and she took me into the Mother Superiors office. I admired the sculpture for a second time and asked Sister Bridget did she know the story of the missing part but she just said;

"I understand some student stole it to get back at the Mother who had given her punishment," so I asked; "Did you know Ellen Daly, she used to work here. Do you know her?" Sister Bridget smiled.

"I heard stories about the mystery of the missing stone and Ellen Daly but they're just stories I understand. I mean I never actually met Ellen Daly," she said. I told her we had been chatting to some people about Ellen and some people think the story is true but we can't find the missing piece or the lady who bought it from Ellen. Sister Bridget said; "If you could find Ellen Daly then she could help."

I just nodded and said nothing.

"Did you ask the Mother Superior here at the Convent, she has been here a lot longer than me? If there was any truth in the story then she might shed some light on it, she's up in the residential area if you want we could go up and see her?" said Sister Bridget.

"That would be great as long as we're not disturbing her or anything and it's ok with you?" I replied. "Nah it's no bother, sure we can ask when we go up and if she is busy then we'll come back another time," Sister Bridget said gathering up some papers, "c'mon then and we'll see."

Off we went up to the residential area; this was the Sisters quarters where they stayed. I guess this was the real Convent if you wanted to call it that. We went inside and Sister Bridget asked me to wait in the hallway. There was a large wooden stair case spiralling up from a marble floored hall, the large wooden doors echoing as the open and closed and the sound of Nuns shuffling around upstairs. Sister Bridget appeared a few minutes later from behind the staircase:

"This way Sarah," she said beckoning to me with her hand. I followed and we arrived at a large wooden door and she pushed it open, the Mother sat behind her desk.

"It's not often we get many visitors in the summer months," she said, "Sister Bridget tells me you've got a question or two for me?" the Mother continued.

I was a little nervous speaking to the Mother. "If it's ok M'am, I'd like to ask you about somebody and something too?" I said, my voice a little shaky.

"Go ahead child and if I can help I will," she replied.

"I'm trying to find out if anybody remembers Ellen Daly; she used to work here a long time ago?"

I asked.

"Yes I remember her, she was an orphan girl who worked here with us after being taken in by the order, she was here from she was a baby up until she was in her early twenties, she was a good hard worker and had the benefit of being brought up by the sisters here but then she made the mistake of being greedy, she stole from the Convent."

The Mother frowned and then went on, "When she was questioned about the incident initially she lied and then said she was paid to do the deed. I had little option but to ask her to leave the Convent and return when she was willing to tell the truth and confess. Also she must return the item she stole from the Sisters."

The Mother got up from the desk; "She left and never returned and neither did the piece. Why do you ask child?" she said turning to me.

"I met a lady who claims she is Ellen and she still claims she is innocent," I said.

"You met her?" replied the Mother with a look of complete shock on her face. "Where?" she continued.

"I can't say Mother as Ellen has asked me not to, I promised with the help of some friends to try and prove she was set up. I'm trying to find the piece of the sculpture and return it. Hopefully we can find the lady who paid Ellen and at least she can prove she was telling the truth," I said hopefully.

"I think you're wasting your time, that's been thirty odd years ago, that piece isn't likely to turn up now. If I was you I'd go and enjoy my summer holidays and forget this whole affair," said the Mother. I thought she might just be right and Sister Bridget and I went back down and finished the weeding around the grounds before I made my way home.

Chapter 12

A few weeks after visiting the Mother the girls and I were still calling to see Ellen and getting the odd progress question from Mrs Thompson, but unfortunately we had nothing to add really and had resigned ourselves to the fact the missing piece and the lady were going to remain just that a mystery. On the second week of August, the mission came to Rosnarene and one of the evening masses was on old Irish beliefs and how they were beginning to get lost in the more modern era. The Missionary asked at the youth mass for the young people to bring an item they thought held some connection with religion from the past if they could find one. I asked Mum had we anything old and religious and Da said, "Take your Granny," but Mum said;

"She might be old enough but she isn't that overly religious, if you hunt in the bottom of the side board Sarah you should get Trina or Shauna's prayer book from their confirmation. That's about fifteen years old now," she said. That would do great I thought as Madonna and Niamh had old Rosary beads and Claire was bringing and old statue that belonged to her Granny before she died. I went into the kitchen and pulled open the door of the side board, about two bags of papers and documents fell out on top of me. After I had gathered up half the rubbish and moved it to the side I was able to see into the side board and the search for the prayer book began. There was everything in here old pictures, leaflets from school concerts, old newspapers and all sorts of stuff. I was rummaging around in the papers when I found a brown paper bag, it was heavy and I thought at last I've got the prayer books but when I opened it there was something wrapped in tissue paper. I sat up at the table and unravelled the paper to reveal a lump of old slate. When I turned it over I got the surprise of my life, on the other side was the doorway to the model of St Frances. I just sat and stared at it, how had it got here? Should I just put it back and say nothing? What am I going to do? All these questions were running through my mind when the kitchen door swung open;

"Did you get them Sarah?" asked Mum.

"Eh, no, not yet. I found this though Mum," I said, holding up the piece.

"What's that? Something you made at Art class?" she said.

"No Mum, this is the missing piece of the Mosaic at St Frances'; the whole village have been looking for this for years and all the time it's been in our side board?" I went on, "A lady got thrown out of the Convent for stealing this piece, so how did we get it Mum?" I asked.

Mum didn't look too concerned; I don't think she understood the serious nature of the find.

"Where did you get that?" she asked me.

"In the side board, it was wrapped in tissue paper and inside this brown paper bag," I replied holding up the paper. Mum sat down at the table, "Where did that come from?" she said scratching her head, "Hold on, your Nana gave me that, I remember now. The time we had the bust up and she left for the sheltered housing, do you mind a couple of year ago now?" Mum looked at me then continued, "That day she was in town and going for the bus she gave me that package and I was that worried about where she was going I came home and threw that into the side board and never even looked at it." Mum stood up and went back into the living room. "Can I take this?" I shouted.

"Aye if it's any good to you," I quickly put the piece back into the tissue paper and into my bag and headed for the park to meet the girls. In the park I couldn't contain the excitement and got everyone gathered round before revealing the missing piece of the puzzle.

"Where did you get that Billy?" asked Claire, "Is that what I think it is?" said Niamh.

"Yes, it's the missing piece; I found it in our house. My Nana gave it to my Mum. Ellen will be pleased now we can finally prove she was telling the truth!" I said looking at the girls, but Madonna said; "Sarah, this must mean your Nana is the lady who paid Ellen to steal it?"

I'd never even thought of that, I was just so happy at finding the piece.

"You're right Madonna, my Nana must be the one but why, and how do I ask her?" I said.

I had a whole new dilemma now developing.

"Hello ladies and what have you got there?" said Mickey Thompson sneaking up behind us. I quickly put the piece away. "It's nothing, mind your own business," I said sharply.

"Keep your hair on pin head I only asked," Mickey replied.

"Go away home and play with your toys," Claire said.

"Shut up, it's quite a big package, maybe it's your lunch?" Mickey sniggered as Colin arrived. "What's the crack today girls, is our boy giving hassle as usual?" Colin said.

"He's like an itch you can't reach, just annoying," was Madonna's reply.

"I think you lot are up to something, you are always fishing round. Firstly in the woods then at the Convent and then at our house, did you find the woman yet?" Mickey said.

"What woman?" I snapped.

"The woman you were talking to my Ma about, I listened to you through the keyhole in our kitchen door." Mickey said smiling.

"He's talking rubbish as usual Billy, he's just trying to see what he can find out. Tel him nothing," said Claire.

"Am I talking crap tubby, alright then how would I know you need to find something and help some old doll that my Ma used to know?" he smirked and went on, "Ask pretty boy there beside you he knows this old doll too," Mickey said nodding at Colin.

"Do you know Ellen?" asked Niamh.

"I went into the woods once and thought I saw a woman and went home. That's all there is to tell," Colin replied.

"Liar!" shouted Mickey, "He went down into the woods and was lifting bits of logs and some old doll ran after him, he nearly pissed his drawers and ran home to our house screaming like a girl! My Mum was telling my Da about it and I was listening."

Colin started towards Mickey; "Come here and I'll give you a good thump!" Colin shouted as Mickey scarpered out the park gate roaring, "I'll bring you up a change of knickers," while he ran for home to safety. Colin came back and started to explain;

"I was down there once and I'm telling you there is a woman down there, I saw her." he said.

"Aye we know Colin we've been going up and down and chatting to her for ages, she is grand. There's nothing to be afraid of, she has nowhere else to go and we're trying to help her," I said, and we all gave Colin a brief run down of the situation so far. After a while we went down to Ellen's. Firstly she gave us the evil eye for bringing Colin down but on closer inspection she said, "Oh you've been here before haven't you?" Colin just stared;

"Yeah, I was down here years ago and you spooked me out Mrs," he said.

"It's Miss" replied Ellen.

"I have something for you," I said unveiling the missing piece.

"My God; it's the piece of the sculpture. I never thought I'd see that again. You've found the lady who set me up then too I take it?" she asked.

"Well I guess we have Ellen, it's my Nana. She was the one who paid for the piece and then denied she knew you. She must be, she had the missing piece after all," I said feeling a little shame.

"Then these are hers," Ellen said handing me the remainder of the golden coins. If you can take them to her and tell her Ellen Daly sent them, then maybe I can finally get some peace of mind," Ellen said. I lifted up the coins and the small purse and we went back up the steps to the top of the embankment. I explained to the girls that I must go and visit Nana tomorrow and sort this out, they offered to come along but this was something I had to do and wanted to do on my own.

Next morning I went on the bus into Rosnarene and got off at the Convent, I saw Sister Bridget and Sister Teresa on my way past and soon I arrived at Nanas. I pressed the buzzer and went in and Nana was watching the television, it was some soap opera and she was glued to it.

"Hello Nana, how are you?" I asked but she never answered, her gaze fixed on the screen.

"That Paul is a nasty piece of work," she said turning to me as the titles rolled. I sat down.

"Nana, I need to talk to you, I need to ask you some questions." I said.

"Fire away I'll give you the benefit of my worldly knowledge," she replied smiling.

"Firstly Nana I have found the missing piece of the Mosaic that's up in the Convent," I revealed. "What do you want a prize? I told you years ago where that piece was, don't you remember I told you I gave it to your Mum?" she said totally unconcerned. Nana got up and walked into the kitchen; "Do you want a drink of juice?" she said as I followed her in.

"I need to know Nana how you got the piece?" I asked.

"That's a good question. It has been a long time, somebody gave it to me, but I can't mind who it was." She studied for a bit, "What's the big deal with anyway?" she asked.

"Nana, a lady stole that piece of the sculpture and sold to another woman, the other woman asked her to steal and she paid her to do it. After it came out about the theft the first lady tried to explain but the second lady denied the whole thing and the first lady got thrown out of the village," I said. "That's as clear as fog, this woman and then that woman and the first woman and the second woman; I have no idea what you're talking about?"

Nana did look confused so I tried again this time more direct:

"Ellen Daly was paid to steal that piece from the convent and then driven out of the village when she was questioned by the Mother Superior. Did you pay her to steal it Nana?" I asked.

"I am many a thing but I'm no crook or thief. Close the door on your way out and I don't expect you'll be visiting me any time soon, as you're no longer welcome."

Nana just walked past me like I wasn't even there.

"Let me explain!" I tried to stop her but she ignored me completely. I went to the door and shouted, "Bye Nana!" but there was no reply. I was very sad. I had accused my own Nana of being a liar and a cheat, add to that the fact I thought she was paying somebody to steal from the Holy Order, but she did have the piece so what do I do now? I went home and as I went in through the back door Mum called out, "Sarah if that's you I'd like to see you in the front room."

I walked in and Mum said; "You've been up to Nana's today?" I nodded.

"She rang to say you called her a thief in her own home. Do you want to explain?" Mum asked. "Mum, I know a lady who was driven out of the village for taking a piece of the St Frances Mosaic, the reason she took it was somebody paid her to steal it. The piece has been missing for thirty years and I found it in our side board. Nana had it and gave it to you the day she left, which means Nana must have been the lady who paid my friend to steal it?"

I was hoping Mum would understand but she just stared; "Why would Nana want to steal something from the Convent?" she asked "Well I thought she might have wanted to get back at them for you not getting a place and that was a way?" I said.

"I am going up to Nanas now to have a wee chat with her, and I'll get to the bottom of this, theft is a very serious matter Sarah and you have made a very serious accusation."

Mum put her coat on and went out the front door. I was very upset and went to my room; I just sat there thinking of Nana and what she must think of me now. I think I cried myself to sleep and when I woke the sun was beaming through the space in our bedroom curtains. I got up and got washed and dressed and went down for breakfast, Mum was in the kitchen and to my surprise so was Nana. "Imelda you may put more eggs and bacon on, If I'm going to be executed for stealing I'm not going on an empty stomach," she said sarcastically as I came in.

"Morning Nana," I said.

"Morning Inspector," she said. I just let it pass and sat down at the table.

"We tracked down where Nana got the missing piece of that model thing, you know the Convent thing," said Mum confidently.

"What, you remember who gave it to you Nana. That's brilliant. Who was it?" I asked excitedly. "Imelda do you hear something in here, it sounds like a child talking," Nana shrugged and turned her back to me.

"Look Nana I was wrong to accuse you and I'm sorry I did," I said shuffling over towards her, "Can't hear a thing," she said so I tried Mum;

"Where did the piece come from Mum, will you tell me?" Mum turned and said;

"Elsa gave it to Aggie; years ago one night on the way home from the bingo." I was lost.

"So where did she get it from then?" I asked but Mum didn't now but said, "I asked your Nana over for a bite of breakfast and thought maybe you and her could sort out your differences eh?"

I looked at Nana but she quickly looked away rolling her eyes up to the sky;

"I'm sorry Nana, I made a mistake and I got it wrong."

I held out my hand and Nana said "You got it very wrong, I never stole anything in my life and I brought my family up the same way as my Mother and Father brought me up. Have respect for people and their property. Elsa gave me that piece of slate years ago and told me it was worth money so I kept it in my safety deposit box at the Post Office I took it and my money out that day I left here and I gave it to your Mother to pass on to you. I know nothing of how Elsa got it or any other lady who stole it. I left it with the only family I've got so if it was worth anything you and your Mother would have the good of it. I paid no-one for it."

Nana shook my hand; "I hope you have learned a lesson from this young lady, get your information straight before you start pointing your finger at people," she said.

Mum sat down the fry up and Nana started to tuck in "I'm really sorry Nana, but I have to find out how Elsa got this piece. Somebody paid for that piece to be taken and it's my job to find out whom?" I did my daily routine in the summer months and went to Claire's and then into the park. There we met up with Niamh and Madonna and the investigation began again.

I explained to the girls how I had asked Nana about the piece of slate and how she reacted so angrily. I told them Nana was very annoyed and told me she got the piece from Elsa her Bingo pal, after much deliberation we decided to go back to Gertie Thompson and see if she could shed anymore light on the case. When we got to the paper shop Gertie was chatting away to customers and when they cleared she turned to us; "Well ladies, how are you lot keeping. How's the detective work coming along?"

I didn't say anything but just set the brown bag on the counter; "What's this then a prezzie for me?" Gertie asked smiling. "Open it" said Madonna. Gertie did as she was asked and then just stood there staring into the package. "Is that what I think it is?" she asked and then went on, "Where did you get it? And better still who is the scoundrel who set up poor Ellen?" she looked at us and Niamh nudged me forward.

"My Nana had the piece, but she said that a friend of hers called Elsa gave it to her ages ago. My Nana was adamant that she didn't pay any one for the slate and so we are at a dead end. Can you help any more?" I asked hoping she'd say yes but she just shook her head.

"Before my time girls. At least you have the piece now to return to the Convent and I bet Ellen was pleased you tracked down the piece too?" she enquired.

"Not really, we got the piece but we still haven't discovered who it was that set up Ellen and at the end of the day it was Ellen we wanted to help?"

I was still in the middle of my explanation when the shop door swung open and in walked Mickey. "Hello ladies, make way for the good looking one," he said winking at Niamh.

"I think I'm going to puke," said Claire. Mickey's Mum started to laugh,

"This is Michaels first day," she announced.

"First day?" asked Niamh.

"First day at what?" added Madonna.

"First day at not acting like a nerd?" Claire chimed in.

"It's Michaels first day at work, he's the new paper boy," Gertie said proudly.

"That's right I'm going to be earning a few quid and who knows what I might spend it on," again Mickey smiled over at Niamh.

"I mean it I'm really going throw up if he doesn't stop," said Claire putting her hand over her mouth. Gertie gave Mickey his route of deliveries and set out his stash of papers and he was ready for the off. "Hold on Michael, you need your bag and jacket," his Mum said.

"My what?"

Mrs Thompson went in behind the counter and came out with a bright Orange bag with the words 'The Independent' emblazoned on it. "There's your bag for the papers and here's your jacket, "she said holding out a bright yellow jacket. It was massive.

"Try it on," she said, Mickey took the jacket and put it on. The sleeves were down over his hands and the jacket was trailing down by his heels.

"It's a wee touch big on you Mickey," said Madonna sniggering. Mickey had a face like thunder; "You'll soon grow into it like," Claire laughed.

"Eh you're funny, looking," shouted Mickey.

"I could get Mr Kelly to see if he has a smaller one when he comes back after dinner time?" said Mrs Thompson.

"I know where there's one, it's on the wee Gnome up in my Aunties garden, and do you want the fishing rod as well?" Niamh joined in, even Gertie had a giggle at that.

"I hate you tramps!" Mickey screamed taking the coat off and firing it into the corner.

"Michael!" shouted his Mum, "You watch your language Mister!"

Mickey turned to his Mum, "I quit!!"

"You haven't started yet so you can't quit," I said.

"Shut up you bowl head freak!" Mickey roared his face red with bad temper.

"Michael, you apologise right now!" his Mum said.

"No I won't do it; they're all making fun of me and that stupid Yellow jacket. I don't want to work here, I hate it already!" Mickey ran out the door with his Mum in hot pursuit.

"Get back here and apologise," she said but Mickey was gone, pedalling down the footpath. Mrs Thompson returned to the shop; "I'm terribly sorry about that, I think he's a little angry," she said. "It's ok, don't worry about it," I replied.

"What do you think we should do now with the slate?" asked Claire.

"I don't know. I would return it to the Convent and ask Elsa can she help, or maybe it would be best to just leave it be."

Gertie didn't seem that bothered either way now;

"You found the piece and maybe that should be the end of it now?" she suggested, but we couldn't just leave it there. Charlie's Angels wouldn't have just stopped with half the case solved and neither should we.

After we left the shop we went back up by Green river and worked out our next move, we would take tomorrow off as we all had different things going on and on Thursday we would go up to Elsa's flat at the sheltered housing and ask her about the slate. Once we had that information we would then go back down to see Ellen and take it from there. On Wednesday our house was full as usual, it was Whitney's second birthday and Trina and Pauric had invited everybody to our place in the evening. The guest list consisted of Nana and Hairy Mary who wasn't so hairy anymore, Eamon, Cassie and Barry, whose teeth had nearly grown back, Shauna and Nicky, Paurics brother Darren with the head that looked like it was on fire and the Aunt who nobody seemed to know. It was the usual Corke family party, Whitney in the middle of the kitchen surrounded by wrapping paper and presents while the rest of the house had guests scattered all over it drinking tins of beer and glasses of God knows what. Mary was in the front room telling everybody the story of the time she waxed her chin and her hearing improved because of it and then Darren started;

215

"I mind a few years ago, I got the old chest waxed to raise money for the Africa appeal, I was squealing like a young piglet. It fair brings the tears to your eyes," he said.

"Did they get much off you? asked Nana?

"Oh jeepers are you codding me, there was enough to make a small rug!" he replied.

"Did they get much money off you, I meant!" Nana snapped back.

"Oh right I can't remember rightly, I just remember having to put cream on my chest for a week to cool it. I was as sore as blind bile." Darren said.

"I tried it out on my chin and I thought I'd taken the skin and all away with it," said Mary.

"You must be doing something wrong," said Shauna. "At the salon where I'm doing my training, ladies come in all the time and have all sorts of things waxed off, and there's never a word out of them!"

Nana looked surprised; "Like what?" she asked.

"Well they do their legs, and their eyebrows sometimes under their arms and other places," Shauna smirked.

"What kind of ladies do you have in the city? They must be running about like hairy peaches, I mind a few years ago when we were chasing the men unless it was a special occasion we kept our winter coats on as long as possible before taking the razor till it?" Mary said looking at Nana for support. "Aye indeed we did Mary and we never had any bother getting the men," she laughed.

216

"I'd say you were a looker in your day?" said Darren spitting on his hands and clapping them together, "I'd have taken you round the floor a couple of times and no mistake." he said.

"Not with a head of mad hair like that you wouldn't," Nana whispered to Mary, and they both burst into cackles of laughter. After the singing of Happy Birthday I took Whitney out for a walk and let the rest of them indulge in the celebrations. We walked about and went to the park before heading back down home. We had a decent tea after the party food earlier and through out the evening the guests made their way home, some of which were a little of the wobbly side.

Thursday morning came and we set off to the sheltered housing to have a chat with Elsa, we brought the slate along to help refresh her memory. I had remembered how I approached this subject the first time with Nana and I wasn't about to get thrown out of another house. I was also able to lavish my previous experience on the others to prevent them suffering the same fate. When we got to Elsa's flat she invited us in and made us very welcome;

"To what do I owe the pleasure of so many visitors?" she asked as she showed us into her small living room.

"We need to ask you some questions Elsa, if that's ok with you like?" said Claire.

"I doubt there's very little I could tell you young ones that you don't already know, but if you want to ask then I'm ready," Elsa said settling back in her arm chair. We didn't say anything at first but just handed

217

her the package, she opened it and said; "Where did you get this?" she looked a little anxious.

"We found that and we have traced back as far as you," I said.

"This is a very tricky situation," said Elsa, "I gave this to a friend of mine years ago and she said she would keep it and make use of it when the time was right. Have you taken it without her permission?" she asked.

"Do you know what it is?" Madonna asked.

"Yes it's a piece of old French art; it was made by some man who is dead now. It's worth a lot of money," Elsa said confidently. We knew she was mistaken but let her talk just to hear were her story was going.

"When I was working down at the quay side as a young woman I met a nice man down there and he was quite taken by me. We hit it off and after we went out for a wee while, he gave me this lovely gift for my birthday." She smiled; "He thought something of me I can tell you. He told me all about the piece and where it come from, and I'll tell you better than that he was a foreigner himself so he would have known the inn's and out's of the whole thing," Elsa looked at us;

"Now my turn to ask a question, where did you get the piece from?"

I stepped forward, "My Nana had it and gave it to my Mum and I found it in the side board of the house."

I paused and looked round the other girls; "I'm afraid Elsa, your boyfriend was telling you a lie. This piece was taken from the Convent at St Frances and the

218

person who took it sold it to a lady who encouraged her to steal it in the first place."

Elsa frowned. "After me and the man split up and went our separate ways, I threw out everything belonging to him, any of the stuff he bought me I dumped, and when I came across the slate I gave it to my best friend at the time Aggie O' Hare. She was married with a young family and would make better use of the money she'd get if she sold the thing on to somebody else."

Elsa paused and then continued, "I thought the damn thing was bad luck any way and I was glad to get rid of it. It's from the Convent, here in Rosnarene, I don't believe you? All these years I was telling people of the handsome foreign sailor I let slip threw my hands as a young thing and all the time he was a lying, two faced old shite hawk."

Elsa was a tiny bit cross; "Hold on a second, where did he get it from then? He certainly was no lady," she said, and she was right. This was getting worse by the minute Nana had been given the piece by Elsa who got it as a present from a foreign guy who worked down at the quays, while Ellen said she sold it to a lady who approached her in town and asked her to steal it? We talked to Elsa for another hour or more but couldn't make anymore headway. After leaving Elsa we went to the usual head quarters, the roundabout in the park.

"This is getting really weird, somebody is telling us a load of rubbish," Niamh said.

"Yeah there has to be somebody spinning us a story, I mean we aren't likely to find a foreign sailor from thirty years ago wondering around the village. I don't know who or what to believe?" said Madonna. I sat there and a million things were racing through my head; had Nana and Elsa cooked up the story between them, would they be that sharp, why didn't anybody mention the sailor before, and what did we really know about Ellen?

"The coins," shouted Claire, "What about the coins? My Uncle said they were French. Do you remember?" Claire was getting excited; "If the coins were French then at least we know Elsa's story checks out, Ellen was paid the French coins and she stole the piece and got the coins in exchange. Simple."

She thought she had cracked it; "Yeah but Ellen said she was asked by a lady or two to steal the piece, she never mentioned a French man or a sailor?" I said.

"This is starting to fry my brain now," explained Madonna. We thought the next best move was to go and chat to Ellen so we went down to the shack in the woods. Ellen was dithering about putting twigs on a small fire and mumbling away to herself and after the formalities we got down to talking; "We've been to see another lady about the slate Ellen but she didn't buy it from you either, or so she says," Niamh asked then Claire said;

"Do you know any sailors?"

Ellen said, "I've heard enough of this, the ones up there are forever making fun, I've been lied to laughed at and cast out for years and now their children are coming down to question me too. Take your slates and coins, and anything else you've brought down here and go away home."

She shuffled over to the shack as I said, "Wait Ellen we're trying to help you not cause any trouble," she snapped back.

"You've been trouble from you came down here, go home and don't come back down here anymore, any of you or I'll put the dog on you." She walked inside and slammed the door shut. We had no option but to leave and go back up to the park and collect our thoughts and start yet again to try and find the answer to a mountain of questions.

A few days before the start of the new term at school the girls and I decided our search was over. We couldn't take the case any further, we had exhausted all the avenues and there was nowhere or no-one else left to ask. We decided it was time to return the piece to the Mother at the Convent and close the case. We went in to Rosnarene and met Sister Bridget in the Convent we explained that we needed to see the Mother as we had something for her, so Sister Bridget took us to the office were the Mother was preparing the work for the new school year.

"Come in girls and sit down, what can I do for you?" the Mother asked.

"Well Mother we have something that belongs to you, well to the Convent and we think you should have it back," I said speaking on behalf of all of us. I held out the package and the Mother took it and opened it; "I don't believe it, my God Lord." She walked across to the mosaic and the piece fitted perfectly into the empty slot.

"I never ever thought I'd see the day that the St Frances Convent model would be complete. Where did you ladies get this piece?" the Mother said turning to face us.

"It's a long story Mother but in a nutshell it was in my house for the past two years, a safety deposit box at the Post Office for 28 years and before that a French sailor had it and gave it to his lover for a present." Niamh explained.

"And how did the sailor get it?" she asked.

"We haven't solved that part yet and I don't think we ever will, so it's best we return the piece to the rightful place and leave the rest to remain a mystery," Claire said, and we nodded in agreement. "That might be the best way girls, you did the right thing returning the piece of the model and you can do no more," said the Mother Superior. We walked back to the bus stop and although we agreed we had did as much as we could; there still was that sinking feeling that we still hadn't solved the riddle of Rosnarene. I was adamant that one day I will find the answer but I didn't know how I could ever get the right answers. In the new school year I was in Sister Margaret's class and choosing my subjects for the next two years ending in my 'O' Level exams, one of my subjects was History and the project was local History. The waterways that were all but finished up now, but used to carry large vessels from all over to the quayside was the main part of our course work before the test papers much further down the line. On one class trip we were taken to the Museum of Transport, there we could see how the river used to be the main source of transport in and out of Finagate and Rosnarene as all the imports came in there and the exports from the Mill went out the same way. We were able to see old log books and old things taken from the boats and barges that would travel along the waterway; the most valuable of all was the old photographs. Niamh, Madonna and I were all in the same class now and I was quite enjoying the research and I was able to ask Elsa, Nana and her friends about the "Good old Days" as they called them. One evening we stayed back after school had finished and were going through our information when Niamh said;

"This is really weird; there are people in these old pictures I know."

She started pointing at the pictures. "Look I know I couldn't know them but they look really familiar."

Madonna and I went over to where she was and looked at the pictures, they were of old boats and crews and people on the quayside taken years before. "I don't know any of them," said Madonna. "Look" said Niamh, she pointed at a lady with a long apron on and her hair tied up in a bun; "I know her from somewhere," Niamh said.

"She does seem familiar, doesn't she?" I said under closer inspection. There was no date on the picture so we couldn't tell that way, after a while the penny dropped; "It's the old lady that lives up at the Convent!" said Niamh in a flash of inspiration.

"Elsa?" I said.

"Yeah, you know the one who used to work down by the Quay; I told you I knew her face!"

Niamh was quite chuffed at finding out she was right and after I had another look I agreed it was in deed Elsa. "I'm taking a photocopy of this and I'll bring it up to the sheltered housing after we finish up," I said going up to the office to copy the pictures.

"You may as well copy them all and then we won't have to stay on here much longer," shouted Niamh. I took all the pictures and made copies and I went around to the sheltered housing as Madonna and Niamh went home. Into Nana's house and the usual suspects were there Mary in the far corner with a bag of Merry Maids on her lap while Nana and Elsa were playing draughts on the table.

"Well girls, how's things with you today?" I asked entering the room.

"Sssssh!" said Nana as she moved closer to the draught board, "I've got you by the you know what?" laughed Elsa.

"Stop it now you're putting me off, between you and Mary sucking and slapping over there what chance have I?" Nana complained.

"You have to jump her, you can't bluff or she'll lift you and when you do jump her she'll take your two crowns and that's you beat," said Mary unwrapping another sweet.

"Oh hello Sarah love I didn't hear you come in," said Nana turning to me, she quickly folded the board closed. "We'll play again later when we haven't got visitors," she said to Elsa. Elsa had a face of complete disbelief while Mary said, "I was waiting to play the winner there."

The board disappeared from sight at lightening speed and Nana directed her conversation at me.

"I didn't expect to see you today, have you missed the bus?" she said.

"Nah Nana, I have something to show you," I said pulling the picture out of my bag.

"Do you know anybody in that picture?" I asked. Nana took the picture and held it about two feet from her face, still squinting she said; "I can hardly see that at all, my eyesight is useless. Do you know any of them people?" she said passing the picture to Mary. Mary closed one eye and had a look.

"There's old McGrath, and Paddy Hayes, do you mind they used to do the loading of the barges, and there's..." she paused, "Is that you Elsa in that picture with the long piny on you?" Mary continued handing the picture to Elsa.

"That's me surely, I was a lot younger then but I haven't changed much." Elsa grinned;

"There's one or two more lines on your dial now Elsa," said Nana.

"More than one or two Aggie, I was only in my early thirties there that was what..." she paused and seemed to be calculating in her head, "About 1952 when that was taken," she concluded.

I had to go on otherwise I would have missed the bus but I left them the copy to reminisce over. I was home, had my dinner and was up in my room doing my

Maths homework when Mum called out; "Sarah, phone for you."

I went down; "Hello," I said.

"Sarah, its Niamh. Do you know them pictures that we were using today?" she asked.

"Yeah, what about them?" I replied.

"Have a look at the one with the boat in the background," she said.

"I can't look at them I left them up in Nana's flat, Nana and her mates were having a good laugh at them. Why what's up?" I asked.

"Do you remember today I said I thought I knew the people in the picture?" I replied, "Yes."

Niamh said; "Well the second one in from the right in the picture is Ellen, Ellen Daly?"

There was a long pause.

"Hello, Sarah. Are you still there?"Niamh asked.

"Eh yes I'm still here. I just don't believe it. Are you sure Niamh?" I asked.

"Yeah it's her alright I knew I knew that face, it's a young picture of her but its her. What are we going to do now?" Niamh said.

"I don't know this is incredible. I have a plan Niamh. I'll tell you and Madonna tomorrow at school and we'll get Claire and take another look at the pictures. Thanks for ringing!" I said and I hung up. The case was back on again another lead had surfaced completely out of nowhere and we had to act on it and I knew just how. After much closer inspection by all four of us at the picture next day I revealed my plan, we

226

would take the picture and some other stuff and watch Ellen's expression and see if it tells us anything.

"Nice idea Sherlock but Ellen doesn't want us anywhere near her place so how do we see her face when she sees the picture?" asked Madonna.

"You leave that to me and meet me here at the convent on Saturday lunchtime," the girls agreed. We couldn't wait for Saturday to arrive and we met promptly at 1:00pm at the Convent.

"What are the plans then Sarah, and why are we here?" asked Claire.

"C'mon I want to show you something," I said leading the way to the sheltered housing.

"What are we doing here Sarah, you know your Nana and the others go into town on a Saturday," said Madonna.

"Yeah I know but just trust me on this one."

We went around the back of Nana's flat and set out some fruit on the bunker and placed the picture among the fruit.

"Over here," I said, pointing to the bins.

We went out of sight; "What, are you waiting for a crow to come down and nick the picture?" asked Claire.

"No just wait and watch."

After about half an hour there was a noise in the bushes at the bottom of the garden and true to form Ellen appeared.

"It's her, It's Ellen!" whispered Claire as we watched Ellen slink up the garden to the stash of fruit. Ellen started loading the fruit into her coal bag then

227

suddenly she stopped and picked up the picture, before when she came up the garden she was gone in an instant but this time she just stood there staring at the picture.

"What do we do?" whispered Niamh.

"Nothing, just watch her," said Madonna. Ellen dropped her bag and started crying as she stared at the picture, I could feel a big lump in my throat as I looked at the others who had eyes all welling up as well. I stood up and Ellen turned quickly but made no attempt to run away again,

"It's you isn't it, in the picture?" I said, but Ellen just stood and wiped her tears away.

"Ellen what's it all about, tell us what's going on and maybe we can help you?"

Ellen crumpled up the picture up in her hand, "It's too late now," she said. She lifted her bag and left, taking the picture with her so we followed all the way to the shack. When we got there Ellen was inside sobbing over the picture.

"What is it Ellen?" I asked.

"This picture, this picture tells it all but nobody can see it only me," she said holding out the picture. "The girl in the picture is me and by my side is that case," she pointed to the small suitcase in the corner. We looked at the picture and could see the case beside the girl. Ellen continued, "I went to the quayside regularly and on one visit I met a man, that man was my Father, the same man that left me at the Convent years before. He told me he came to the quayside every few months and would come up into town and check that I was doing ok but could never speak or make himself known to me."

Ellen was very upset, "He told me that my mother had gone and he couldn't care for me as a child but was ready to take me back. We would need money and if I could get something from the Convent of value then he could sell it on his trip and we could then move away."

We listened intently as Ellen poured out her life story; "I was always told the model in the Convent was priceless and so I took a piece, it didn't matter any piece and gave it to my Dad. He told me on the next trip we would both be leaving and I got ready he came back and we would be leaving within a few days. That's when this was taken," Ellen unravelled the picture again and looked at it. "I went to the Convent and was questioned by the Mother about the piece, I couldn't tell her where it was so I got thrown out, I went into the village to meet Gertie but the word spread and I wasn't welcome anywhere but it didn't matter I was leaving with my Dad."

Ellen sobbed again "I stayed down in the woods for a day or so and went back to the Quayside but Dads boat was already gone. One of the men there gave me a purse and inside were 12 coins and a note saying sorry."

I was starting to cry just listening to Ellen's story;

"My life was over; I had no friends, no family and a village that disowned me. I went to the Mother and told her the story but replaced my Dad with some local ladies but she wouldn't believe me," Ellen paused.

"What about the ladies you told us about that set you up?" Claire asked.

"It's all been a lie, my whole life has been a lie." she said.

"So why are you still here, why didn't you just leave Rosnarene behind and start a new life somewhere else?" I asked.

"Well," said Ellen, "A few days later I was down at the quayside and I saw the lady with the piece of the model I had taken, I knew my Dad had given it to her and I thought one day he'll return to her and when he does I'll be waiting." She looked at us;

"I guess he isn't coming now eh? I have had my case packed for over thirty years and waiting. I kept the purse and the coins until you came along and I thought just maybe he may have returned by now and you could find him, so I gave you the coin so he could see it and know I'm still waiting but he won't come now."

I hugged Ellen and so did the others. She had been so alone for so long waiting and hoping everyday and nothing.

"There's been the odd person down this way but generally I'm on my own apart from Sheba, and even she isn't mine. About ten years ago she wondered down here and she had been hurt, must have been knocked down or something and I took her in and fixed her up as best as I could. I didn't have a name for her but I remembered one night up at the fete in town Gertie Gates and I met a couple and they had a beautiful big dog and the name stuck in my mind, Sheba the lady called the dog and that's where you got that from," Ellen smiled patting the old dog on the head.

"There has always been just me and her and that's the way it's going to stay. It's too late to change things now." Ellen lay down on the pile of old clothes and started to doze a little still clutching the picture. We left quietly and shut the shack door; up in the park we were sitting our eyes red with crying.

"What's up with you freaks, have you been welding without a mask on you or are you all just rubbish at doing your make up?"

It was Mickey Thompson as usual trying to stir up some badness but nobody was in the mood and after a couple of more goes he gave up and let us alone. We all pitched in ideas as to what we do now I suggested going to the Nuns with the new found information. Niamh agreed and said we should try and get Ellen into a house or flat. Madonna suggested we should raise some funds and help her back into he community that way and Claire was willing to do anything to help. We all had pretty sleepless nights and on Sunday went down to Ellen's armed with our suggestions for help. When we got there Sheba was tied up at the shack which was strange but inside was worse, the suitcase, the coins and clothes were gone, and so was Ellen Daly.